Carolin Window gr[illegible] her wanderlust she eventually washed up in Cairns, far North Queensland, where she discovered boats. She is currently working on boats in the Coral Sea and Great Barrier Reef and writing a new novel. *Dim* is her first published novel.

DIM

CAROLIN WINDOW

VINTAGE

FOR TRACEY, MICHAEL AND JANE,
WHO SHELTERED ME AT STRATEGIC POINTS ALONG THE EASTERN COAST OF AUSTRALIA DURING THE MIGRATORY PERIOD WHICH PRODUCED THIS BOOK, AND GAVE UP THEIR SPACE SO I COULD WORK.
THANK YOU FOR HOUSING VAGABOND ME.

THANK YOU ALSO TO JENNIFER, WHO INSPIRED THE DESIGN FOR DIM'S TATTOO.

A Vintage book published by
Random House Australia Pty Ltd
20 Alfred Street, Milsons Point, NSW 2061
Sydney New York Toronto
London Auckland Johannesburg
and agencies throughout the world
First published 1996

National Library of Australia
Cataloguing-in-Publication Data
Window, Carolin.
Dim.
ISBN 0 09 183210 1 (pbk.).
I. Title.
A823.3
Designed by Yolande Gray
Typeset by Midland Typesetters, Victoria
Printed by Griffin Paperbacks, Adelaide
Production by Vantage Graphics, Sydney
Illustrations by Carolin Window

Part One

DIM

1 The Dream

Can I show you the place where I came from? I barely know it myself, since I have only been there in dreams.

When I am deep in the shadow valley sleep, I look over my shoulder into the funnel and the sands run backwards taking me with them. Back upstream; following the winding road like a needle inoutin across the creek nine times. Was this the same needle that once stitched up the lips of the past, and embroidered closed the eyelids that wanted to look back there?

Perhaps. But now it is threading close to the core of things, and we go deep down in the forest, into the cleft of the land where all the trapped energy banked up like fallen leaves, down into the place where I was conceived, not for want of trying.

But you're coming into the dream. Wait a moment. Before you come down there with me to the land where Morgan was queen, you must be ready. The needle is in my hand. So close your eyes up tight, and let me work my needle to knit them safe. Now you see through my eyes, and see as I see. While we're at it, I'll stitch your lips up too. Don't speak—it's my turn. Because this is my dream, I will speak for everyone in it. I am the ventriloquist, throwing each voice into your waiting ear. We'll leave that ear unstitched, so listen.

Morgan and Con came to the valley after they were married, to live in a timber house thickly encircled by rainforest. Morgan liked being deep in amongst the forest because she believed the trees gave her energy. Con hated the trees. To get away from them, he went to town every day to work in the supermarket.

For nine years Morgan and Con were childless.

For the first three years Morgan was convinced that her womb, though slow, was simply biding its time and stewing on the most wondrous fruit, a child which would light up the world when at last it came. She felt her body ripening along with the burgeoning overarching forest, whose insistent expansion began to subsume the house itself. Only the walls separated the preparation within from the proliferation without. When the house grew so shaded and surrounded that staghorns found purchase along its outside, moss rolled luxuriant mats along the porch floor, and creeping vines began to thrust inquisitive tendrils into cracks in the timber cladding and grope their greedy way across the ceilings inside, she refused to let Con cut anything back. No, she would protest calmly, the forest is getting ready.

For the next three years, Morgan watched the rainforest surge and lour around her until she grew so bloated with resentment of its casual plenty that she looked pregnant. In town, people began stopping her in the street to congratulate her. On the last day of that three years, Morgan lost her temper (some said her mind). She put on her gumboots, rolled up her sleeves and went outside to the back porch. She got the axe and began chopping down trees.

By the time Con got home from work she had cleared a space around the house the size of a playing field. When he drove around the corner in their battered Holden, the gravel spitting under the tyres like a firing squad taking potshots at him, he confronted her squatting exhausted in a suddenly treeless clearing surrounded by butchered stumps, the axe blunt in her scabby palms.

—Lord, Morg, was all he said as he slammed the door of the ute and stood surveying the littered cadavers of trees everywhere. After a moment, he went behind the back porch and got the chainsaw, and began to neatly dismember the fallen in a howl of noise and fumes. This took two days. The next day, he built the woodpile, bigger than the house itself, which was to last them the next seven years. Morgan watched him piling up the wood and stated, You know, I would have kept going but the bloody axe got too blunt.

Con didn't reply. He didn't tell her that the shearing down of all those incredible trees, and lord knows how old they were (could have been there a thousand years or more), was like the razing back of six oppressive years. He couldn't have told her that the astonishing new open space, in which their house floated like an island, made the breath rush easy in his lungs. All that space reminded him of the coast where he'd grown up. Every day when he got up and looked out to see the forest held at bay a good distance from the house, he sighed with relief. A man might have a ghost of a chance, he thought, to father a child without all that shade hanging over him, all those trunks and limbs and twigs crowding round him, all those roots spreading under him, all those leaves piling up and rotting against the roof walls even floor of the house.

A ghost wasn't enough for Morgan. She wanted more certainty than a ghost of a chance. Having expended her resentment on the passive sap of the forest, she turned her mind to solutions. I don't know what she did then, not completely. I know she consulted with higher powers. There was a man in town who primed her with potions and instruction in fertility rituals. In the drawer next to the bed she kept an almanac of dates and times, covered with his annotations and her own cryptic marks. She watched the moon, she measured her temperature, she marshalled Con to her rites. This magic worked. After two years and three months I was conceived, and in due course born.

A child so tardy should perhaps have been loved even more because of the long years it took to brew it up. A child born of more than passion: a child fashioned from determination, science, perhaps magic, and ultimately obsession. But by the time Morgan managed to start me, her fantasy of herself as mother was utterly exhausted. Only her bloodymindedness had kept her going all those years, and her concentration on the process had so completely sublimated the notion of its product that a result, so long in coming that it had become unlooked for, was almost an insult to her dedication. Trying to conceive had become a lifestyle, and being a parent was a future quite dissociated from the one she had grown used to.

Morgan's pregnancy was an occupation of sorts. She lived as if possessed by an evil spirit. The morning sickness half killed her. It was harder than anything she had had to endure during her fertility treatments. She retched and retched. Her long black hair was slimed with vomit, and her throat was rough and corroded. She watched her stringy body expand, first with surprise, finally with a feeling edging on horror. There was something obscene in it, she decided.

An odd fear formed in her. The fear that she'd gone against nature. Nature had kept her separate, refused her conception. And now that she was pregnant she was being punished. Punished for what? Punished perhaps for all the things she had done to push this idea of a baby into some semblance of reality. She'd forced this idea to take on flesh and blood. She knew she'd stretched the rules. There had been untruths, secrets and corruptions. Not even Con knew about everything she'd done.

The birth was a nightmare. Even the midwife remarked that it was the most difficult she had seen in many years. Her mouth aching open in screams and her brain buried under the avalanche of the red flowers of pain, Morgan begged forgiveness for her transgressions. She knew that she wasn't forgiven, otherwise the baby would have died and the punishment would have ended there.

That was why, when she finally brought me to light, she took rather a dim view of me. She wasn't the kind of woman to take her punishment lying down.

—What shall we call her, Morg? I mean, something symbolic, something that really shows how much we wanted her, how long we tried, how special she is . . . Con held me, the quiet child with the wormy limbs, as close as he could because he was so happy. Desiree perhaps? Or something to do with a jewel maybe, like Pearl . . . ?

Did Morgan turn her back then? To stare through kamikaze corpses of countless insects stuck on the window, out at the urgent convoluted green just drinking up the darkness of that evening, soaking it up like paper towel blackening with ink and say, with the nightmarish concision which was her trademark.

—No, we'll call her Dimity. Dim for short.

The question was—did Morgan curse me? She called me after the darkness: Dim.

I took the hint. She got it wrong though, a slip of the tongue. What she meant to say was dumb. An easy enough mistake. I got her drift anyway. I didn't speak until I was six years old, and even that was an accident.

It wasn't the first. It was one in a string of accidents. From early on, death loved the little baby Dim that was me, and wanted her for a playmate. As if life, having won the right to bring me forth, had spent itself in that adversity, and had only a loose hold on me. Every now and then, death would get a grip on the scruff of my neck and try to take me back again. Life won out, after a struggle.

Sometimes Morgan didn't know whose side she was on—life's or death's. She regarded me as the child of darkness. This was confirmed when I failed to develop speech. I became the child of silence. I think there was at least once when she offered me up to death, gave death the option of me.

Can I remember as far back as early infancy, as far back as my first month of life, when Morgan bathed me every night by the fire? Or is this a tale that Con told me so often, hanging on his knee like a wind chime bobbing on air, jouncing me up and down and laughing at his baby that loved death so much that it was all he could do to keep her there with him, her own daddy, that it has become my memory?

When the firelight ate up the walls around, bit chunks out of them and retreated so that they regenerated, Morgan would heat the water and pour it into the little laundry tub.

Lowered in Morgan's hold, a fragile cargo, I am like a clay doll, animated. Mine are slow-motion movements, like time-lapse photography of plants coming into flower. Every gesture an unfurling. When my hands clench and unclench it is as delicate and drawn out as a breath.

With motherly tenderness does Morgan dunk me in the water, just lukewarm and waiting for me?

Her hands ladle and channel the water. I am silent, smiling, and the world is cradled in the arc of time as I quiver and undulate in the very centre of it.

Is Morgan distracted? She lets go.

The world comes down on me. The sides of the cradle cave in when time's bow is released, puncturing it and sending me shipwrecked under the world. The breathing turns to water and there is a tide which flows into my lungs and my tiny trembling gut. Purple and at peace now, I am sleeping in my new cradle inverted beneath the sea where the quiet fish welcome me and death swims over and presses me close, in the bosom of the end.

Except for Con. Two knotty hands like old ropes which loop under me and haul me up and back into the air. The cradle, tipping and transforming again in a sudden takeoff as I am airborne. He's patting my back, urgent, slapping the breath back into me, crying himself before I open the clam of my too silent mouth and wail with surprise.

—What the hell do you think you're up to, Morg? A bit of care, eh? A bit of care! The kid's only a month old and you're trying to teach the poor bugger to swim?

Morgan says nothing. She stokes the fire. She looks over Con's shoulder to where I am looking too. Both of us watch death breasting the cold draught coming under the door. Sidling under the door, the visitor is gone.

The fact that I didn't speak proved it. It proved that somehow, a curse was operable here.

The first phase of the curse was the nine years where it seemed no child would come. When she did come, she was somehow not right. This was confirmed when the curse entered its second phase, and it became obvious that this child could not, or would not speak. She cried like any other, she laughed sometimes. But speech would not take root in her.

Even before this became apparent, Morgan was suspicious of me. Now that her major goal in life had been achieved, now that she had performed the impossible and brought forth a child, she was forced to train her obsessions elsewhere. And like all else in Morgan's mind, these obsessions were formidable and difficult ones, and held the potential for extraordinary destruction.

Though it was clear to Morgan that I was damaged, marked in some way for a negative fate, I could not be written off as a changeling. That pregnancy had been notable for the incessant scrutiny of everyone involved. What malicious fairy or devil could have got close enough to substitute its spawn for the perfect baby Morgan should have had? Someone out of the phalanx which attended Morgan would have detected them and their nasty trick. No, Morgan was forced to admit to herself, her baby wasn't a changeling. But there was no reason why Morgan's baby couldn't be a mistake of another sort altogether, an expression of something unnatural. The result of a sin.

You know that Morgan's name goes back to the times before Christianity, right back to Morrigan, the

Irish queen of the elves, who was associated with nightmares and the demon incubus. Now this heritage began to preoccupy her. Every night, nearly, she rehearsed it in some form or other.

Did I hear her say to Con, when I surfaced from my dreams, Listen to her Con. Listen to her.

—She's only dreaming, darl.

—She's laughing.

—So?

—I hate the way she laughs in her sleep.

—Why?

—It's not right. She laughs like a whore.

—Lord, Morgan, she's only a kid.

—My mum always said that when a child laughs in its sleep, the demon Lilith is playing with it.

—The demon Lilith?

—The queen of nightmares and sinful dreams. She comes to kids in their sleep and makes them laugh like that. Not just kids. Grown men too. She uses them create demon hosts.

—You believe this stuff?

—I don't know. I just can't stand the laughing. Can't you stop her laughing?

—Isn't it bad luck to disturb a dreamer?

—Look, I just don't know. Just stop her laughing, Con. It's wrong.

Morgan thought I gambolled at night with demons. Naturally, since she'd also begun to think that I was the offspring of her own union with some dark fantasy, an incubus, that she had entertained when Con was at the supermarket. In my thoughts, I begged her to remember that though these children are supposed to be the deformed ones of this world, they are also the exceptions of any sort. Merlin himself is reputed to have been born of such warped parentage. I may be a freak but I have power. My touch is magic. See my hands, Morgan, they're crooked as a witchdoctor's. And I'm not averse to pointing the bone. Once in a while, I test my power.

Con went away. Before he left he told me about the waves lined up along the coast like gigantic blue glass rissoles. You could get right inside them and rocket through there as if you had wings. He crouched, arms akimbo, to show me. He grinned into the spray. I'd never seen the sea. Con promised to take me with him one day.

While Con was away, the unrest in that place escalated. Our nightworld ruled. I walked in my sleep, waking every time at the foot of Morgan's bed, where she elaborated on her own dream kingdom. Morgan never slept sweetly. Some nights she made so much noise she woke me up. When I went to look at her, I could see her dreams hanging over her head. In the dreams was a white shroud, and that was the ghost which haunted Morgan. The white shroud had big white hands to match. These held knives and scissors and tweezers and odd round glass dishes and tubes. Morgan lay back. She opened her mouth to receive the morsels offered. Her legs flexed under the sheets. She cried a little. There were incantations at her bedside and she was saying her share even though I could see by the pleating at the edge of her lips that she was scared. Scared of what? That the spell might not work? Or that the spell was the wrong spell? Or maybe that the spell was a sin in itself?

Sweat twinkled across her upper lip. She was twitching in her sheets, and her hands caressed empty air whilst at the same time rebuffed it, protested, then tumbled limply down.

Once she ricocheted to a sitting position and cried, Sin! The third is sin!

Her big black eyes were wide open, and they were pronged all around by eyelashes like spears. She glared at me, though she didn't see me. She held her stomach as if she had tummyache. The dreams could be deciphered. Morgan was scared of the phantom because of his touch. There were side effects which she feared. Not just my silence, the obvious side effect which was her daily torture. Physical side effects. I know this because I watched her. There was nothing else for me to do during those long days. I knew that every month she felt her breasts, tremulously, to see if death had taken up residence there yet. She palpated her belly, looking for the sign of the end. There was a stripe going across the base of it, so I always expected that when the end came it would simply prise open the stripe and step forth, the conqueror. I saw her train mirrors between her legs, craning her neck anxiously. Once she caught me looking, and laughed harshly.

—Do you know how you were born? she demanded, eyebrow cocked. Not through here, Dim.

They cut you out like you cut pictures out of magazines for collage, cut you out and stuck you in my arms. Just like collage.

She fretted about the afterlife. She read all sorts of books about it. She said strange prayers, collected plants from the forest and burnt them, dried them, steamed them. There came a time when Morgan decided that the afterlife was not a possibility. I came upon her crying her black eyes purple in the shade of the porch. The sobs were so deep I worried that her insides had splintered. I could hear them cracking. She lifted her head back so that her neck was all exposed, and cackled.

—All this for what!

By the time Con came back she had started to go into the forest. Every day she disappeared into the cave where the forest opened up, briefly, into the clearing. I did not know what she did there, but she came back dirty, her eyes glowing, red mud under her fingernails.

Once I followed her. I saw her moving fast between the leaves ahead. She was as nimble as any animal in that place. In the light her face looked green when she turned to look behind herself. Unexpectedly, she stopped and bent over the ground. I was moving so quickly that I couldn't stop before she perceived me. She whirled around, her eyes pronged again, searching me out.

—Is it Dim, then?

She jumped up. There was a spray of mud as she came running at me. She chased me back the way we had come. The trees crowded around and she gained on me, but I was able to make the clearing. I burst out into the air. Morgan burst out too. She paused at the edge of the cave, swaying.

—I will not be followed. I will not.

She turned back and dived into the cave again.

Con came out of the house, perplexed. That night he asked Morgan why she'd chased me.

—I don't like her following me around. She gives me the creeps. All eyes and no voice.

—Morg, she's your daughter. It's not her fault she can't speak.

—Whose fault is it then?

—No one's. That kind of thing is never anyone's fault.

—It's not what I wanted. A deaf and dumb child. I didn't go through everything I went through to have a deaf mute baby. Better to have given up.

—She's not deaf.

—How do you know?

—Because she listens. You can see her listening. She registers sounds. No problems there, Morg. This little kid can hear as good as anyone.

Morgan was crying. She had tears tracking down her face in the soft light. Con cradled her in his arm. He kissed her mouth, her shoulders, her neck.

—Why were we cursed?

—There's no curse. We were lucky to be able to have a kid of our own. It took a lot and we did it.

—But dumb, Con. Dumb. Missing something.

—She's just a slow learner. Don't worry, she'll talk when she's ready. Ssh now, Ssh.

Morgan didn't believe him. She'd made up her mind about me. I was four years old and well established as her personal curse.

Con was right that I listened. I listened so hard my ears grew pointed. Every evening, Morgan massaged them and taped them down before I went to bed, in the hope of arresting them before they became the unmistakable ears of an elf. In the mornings, she greased them with an ointment that she made herself.

You couldn't stop a kid from listening though.

I listened to the cicadas. I deciphered the long conversations of the winds, which rasped in the gossiping trees, and panted past our house, nicking splinters as they went and strapping the shingles until they squeaked. I listened to the rain, pinging onto the roof so loudly that Morgan couldn't make herself heard. There was thunder that came with it, stamping from far away to tantrum right over our house. At night there were flying foxes raking sounds through fruiting trees, frogs, crickets, wild pigs, feral cats spatting, the strangled croaks of geckoes and the squeals and grunts of the koalas, chasing each other through the bush. When Con saw my head lift as they squalled nearby, he laughed and said, Lecherous buggers. Morgan requested that he did not corrupt the child. That was me that she meant.

There was a stream that talked, and several rocks which did too. And there were birds, always competing.

Their voices bells, cracking whips, whistles, rattles. You couldn't always see them. When the rain came they dipped and whirred through the valley—they loved to show themselves when it was cloudy and wet. They preened in the clearing, and packed it with sounds.

Con took me walking in the forest. It was dark in there. Everything was wet. And it was crowded. Mosquitoes sang over us in clouds. There were so many squelching crackling flapping sodden sounds which our gumboots could call up.

When we were deep inside, the palms closed over our heads and the tall trees closed over their heads. The world was piggybacking itself—when Con lifted me to his shoulders I could see all the trees doing it too. There were huge ferns and staghorns cupped up there in the branches, nesting in moss. And there were vines threading everything together.

—Are you scared, Dimmy?

I wasn't scared.

—No? That's good. I am sometimes. As if you couldn't stand still for five minutes, without all this forest claiming you for its own. Grows so bloody fast.

He listened. There was a multitude of bird sounds stirring the undergrowth. Every type of bird I had ever listened to must surely be here in this part of the forest. Con grinned. He kept walking. And then he stopped suddenly, lightly lifting me down from his shoulders and squatting, holding me against his chest. His finger showed me where to look.

There was a bird. A brown bird the size of a hen,

but with a tail. The tail was brownish too, and ill-assorted—its feathers did not match. But they were shapely, arched and curled like a flourish. The bird's beak was open. I saw what Con meant. This bird was making itself a nest of sound. It was scratching about in a pile of debris, testing all manner of sounds, as if trying to work out which was the best basis for building the nest. It tried the kookaburra, the cockatoo, the whip bird. It didn't stop there. Voice after voice, immaculately rendered, came effortlessly out. This bird was very smart.

Con's gumboot squelched noisily where it slid in the red mud. The bird's eye fixed us, and then the bird ran. Its bland colouring made it invisible almost at once.

Con winked. See? That's the liar bird.

I could see why it was called that. I smiled.

—It can do any bird sound it hears. Sometimes it does other sounds too. Once I heard one do a chainsaw, not long after your mother cleared the area around the house. You know it's there when you hear too many calls. They start to be inconsistent with each other. It's not often there's that many different types of birds hanging out in the one little patch of forest, is it? It can't help itself, see. It gets carried away, like most people. It blows its cover by being too much of a showoff. A virtuoso.

He slapped a mosquito, grimacing. Did I tell you how it got its name?

He shooed more mosquitoes away from my face. No? Well it's because of its tail, which is shaped like a lyre.

I was confused.

—A lyre is like a harp. An old-style instrument with strings. You hold it up like this, and you pluck the strings so you get the sound. Like what the angels play in the pictures of heaven. Understand?

I nodded. So the bird wasn't a liar after all. It was a musician. And a kind of angel.

—Do you reckon that bird wakes up in the morning and has trouble remembering who he is? Do you think maybe he does all those other calls because he doesn't have a call of his own? Could be this is a bird with an identity crisis, eh Dimmy? Don't know what that means, do you?

I shook my head.

—You're too young to know what that is, kiddo. Comes with age. Come on, let's get back. If I stay in here any more I'll end up with a staghorn in each armpit and moss up my nose.

We laughed all the way back to the house.

For the rest of the night I couldn't sleep. I listened feverishly to the outside sounds, wondering which of them were real and which were the theatrics of the lyrebird. The bird inspired and fascinated me. I longed so much to learn to speak after I heard it telling those stories. I recognised a curious and wondrous power in it. From that day, I wanted to be a storyteller too. I longed to be the mistress of many voices, just like that special and celestial musical bird.

2 My Tongue

I sat outside with the jacaranda blossoms spattered all over me, and watched Morgan taking the things off the line. She had grass seeds sprayed all over the backs of her legs. Con had been gone so long that the lawn hadn't been mowed and the grass was at knee height.

The dolls were in a circle, and they watched me with aphid eyes. They were waiting to move and speak and have their party, but they weren't going to let me in on it. When I wasn't looking, I knew they'd start. I was determined this time to catch them at it so I sat in their circle and watched. I wanted them to teach me how to do the talking.

I heard Morgan snort at the line, and say disparagingly to herself, Stupid kid can't even work out how to play with dolls. She turned her back and pulled the pegs out of the towels strung up before her, tossing them in the basket at her feet.

Back under the jacaranda, something was happening though, and all the dolls were wide-eyed with surprise. It went round their little circle like a liquid blue hoop thrown up to the sky. Because little BabyLove, with the perfect cupid's bow puckered up to receive her special bottle, had a new tongue. And she seemed to have forgotten the rules, for she was rolling it around her pearly teeth and letting it lick up her peaches and cream complexion. The dolls all stared in horror at these indecorous tricks, and that made BabyLove stick out her tongue still further because she'd come unstuck, she was past caring about the rules any more and brazen she flaunted them and showed me how it was done.

Then, even more astonishingly, her tongue extended itself still further and, detaching itself from her, it came to me. Did I hear it say *I am yours*? I reached out two arms to welcome it and laughed with delight.

It was the laugh that made Morgan look around from behind a shuddering white wall of sheet and come screaming out of her own world into mine with the garden shovel swept up en route cudgelling the air, her crude voice yodelling as if out of a time tunnel, Dimity don't moooove!

She swooped down on the coiled piece of the tongue which BabyLove had given me and began to rain blows upon it. But it was too swift, too sleek and graceful and articulate. Before she could batter it, it was gone. Sweating and nauseous, Morgan sank down on the dry pebbly patch of ground at the roots of the jacaranda tree, resting her shoulders against it.

There was an explosion as tears found her. And then speech, incoherent, racing raggedly out, Con you bastard your fault that the grass is so long it's a fit home for it when the bloody hell will you come back you're no better just another damned snake in the grass our daughter nearly bit by a *snake*.

—Morgan, don't . . .

Morgan's eyes went wide as BabyLove's and just the one time in her whole life she had nothing, nothing to say. Because she was too surprised to speak. And then she managed this reproof.

—Call me Mum. You don't call your parents by their Christian names.

It was lucky, wasn't it, that when she came running at my tongue with anger and fear and weaponry, that it came inside me to stay, instead of fleeing forever? I saw the snake slide into the purple flecked emerald centre of our knee-high lawn. But before it went it gave me, at the age of six, a voice of my own.

And not long after that, a mirage came and stood at our door. When Morgan turned the porch light on, she discovered it to be my father.

—Where the hell have you been?

—The beach.

—Doing what?

—Surfing. Move over, Morg, where's little Dimmy?

—Hello, Con.

And while Con was staring in delight, his tanned face cracked with a big beautiful grin of amazement, Morgan snapped, Will you never learn? Call him Daddy, you silly kid.

Con had only been talking to me for five minutes before I got sick.

—Dimmy, love, are you all right?

—What's wrong with her? Morgan came out of her book and frowned at me.

—She's swimming. Look at her, she can't hold her head up properly. Dimmy? Dimmy, what is it?

I had the roll and surge of a toxic dream to occupy my eyes, which fluttered half shut while I strayed close to someone I hadn't seen for a while, someone I recognised even though now we were on land and the cradle was outgrown, someone who had always cared for me and sought me still.

—Wait on a minute, Morg, did that snake have a go at Dimmy or not?

—I didn't see it bite her. She reached out for it and . . .

—But did you check, did you have a close look at her and make sure?

—No.

He caught me just as I fell, saying, Hello.

—Who's she talking to?

—No one, Morg, she's delirious.

But Morgan knew, she knew whom I greeted. And where I was, in death's embrace once again, with the furred edges on every shape respirant, reticulate. Death's hand patting my stomach nauseous with poison and the huge violent surge of colours newly slathered onto reality while I swooned on Con's lap and he checked every limb until he found it, the little pinprick mark on the heel of my left foot where the speech had come into me, the poison had found me and the snake had kissed me ready for death to befriend me.

—Look! he exclaimed. Look, here it is. The rotten thing's bitten her.

He rolled me up in a sleeping bag and took me out to the ute. The surfboard was still strapped to the tray. He yelled out to Morgan, through the driver's window, jammed open since the day I was born, I'm going into the hospital.

The hospital knew me. They'd played a part in the making of me and they were there when I arrived into the world for the first time. They knew how to tether me to life, because they'd already done it before. They did it again. The next day, I came back to the forest with Con.

Once the snake gave me my voice I was able to develop other talents. Did I learn from the cicadas?

When I was outside at dusk, the cicadas further down the valley would drone in one long ecstasy of sound. The cicadas up on the hill would find the same pitch, and the sound would go stereo. From two different directions, the same euphoric chirp came pulsing at me. The two currents coming from either end of the world caught me up between them, squeezed me there as they fused and left me hanging up in a crease in time and space as if caught on a string. Just the one bead, me, strung up there in a new and empty universe, vibrating with sound.

I noticed that Morgan, when the cicadas found their frequency, would quickly go inside, muttering one of her superstitious prayers. In the evenings I stayed outside, waiting. I longed to go to that place where my mind hummed and nothing else existed but the seed sound.

I found that if I put the image of the spiral serpent in the space at the front of my mind, like a meditation, I was able to make sound come from the other side too. This had a few uses. I could make Morgan go inside by conspiring with a single bank of cicadas.

But the best thing was that I managed at last to make the dolls speak to me. The snake showed me how to prise open those prim buds of their pursed lips and put voices there. We could sit around under the jacaranda or at the core of the monstera deliciosa or up behind the palms and hold elaborate conferences.

When Morgan found out her anger was like gravel rash—smarting and burning with an incendiary glare of mercurochrome. She smacked me. But she couldn't stop me.

—Con, she'd complain, the child's a devil.

—What?

—I came round the end of the yard the other day and found her talking for her dolls.

—Morg, any kid talks to her dolls. That's what they're for.

—No, she's talking *for* them, projecting her voice, throwing her voice like those comedians with the puppets, you know, the voice comes out of somewhere else, and they don't move their lips?

—Ventriloquists, you mean?

—Yes.

—Good on her then, that's pretty good for a six

year old who's only been speaking three months.

—Con, it's not right.

He changed the subject.

—Morgan, I think we'd better send Dimmy to school now, don't you? She talks as well as any other kid, and she should be ready for it. But since she's a bit delicate, I think we should send her to the nuns. What do you reckon?

Morgan started with surprise. Had she grown so used to me as her own private obsession that the idea of me going independently into the world was too bizarre? Perhaps she was afraid of what I might do, her strange child let loose on the world. She must have decided it was time for the world to have a go at me because, the next week, I started school.

3 The Red Flowers

There was only one piece of information which I learned in primary school that I was able to apply to my real life. It wasn't something the nuns gave me. It was Lachlan Albemarl who told me.

I had a special relationship with Lachlan Albemarl. He tyrannised me. Right from day one, he picked me out, and for the rest of my primary career he backed me against walls and trees with his best scary stories, refined his tortures upon my body, and perfected new technologies upon me. I was his familiar, separate to the roving gang of boys which oscillated around him. But it was me who enabled him to trial and develop the manifold skills which made him a playground icon. He pioneered everything on me. I knew I was special, and I submitted.

On this day, he had just given me a Chinese burn and was squatting in the dust, dividing his attention between a lizard that he was disembowelling with scientific interest, and a pile of spit wads that he had prepared and regimented along the bench ready for the next class.

The cicadas in the playground were firing sound. I sat on the bench, dreaming along its current. I ignored

Lachlan at all times; that was how he liked it. I never sought him, he sought me. He liked the bland accepting face that I presented to his attacks.

Lachlan looked up. He had a huge piece of snot on his finger. He held it out.

—Look!

I came back out of the current. Slowly though. Too slowly for Lachlan.

—Hey! Look!

He thrust the specimen close to my face. I looked. I realised a reaction was necessary. I opened my mouth, searching until I found, Wow!

He was satisfied. He pulled his finger back, scrounged again in the dust, finding the lizard's tail loose there. It was still wriggling. He twisted it back and forth, then said, Were you listening to the cicadas?

I nodded.

—You know when they all do it together and it gets into your head? Well when they do that they get so happy they piss themselves. And if you're walking in the bush when that happens you see this amazing shower of yellow rain. A golden shower—d'you know what that is?

—No.

—Stupid.

To finish the topic, he fired one of the spit wads right at me at close range. It pinged into the centre of my forehead and stuck there, like the marking of the third eye on a deity. Sitting crosslegged, noncommittal, it became me. I left it there until he picked it off when the bell rang. He didn't want the other kids to realise that the ambush was in store.

Lachlan showed and told me other things but I forgot them if I could. The one that took the most forgetting happened on the last day of primary school. I managed the forgetting, but there were simple things which brought it back. Like red flowers.

The red. There was so much red. It was not just the red of the poinciana tree blossoms falling all around in the high wind. It was the red where Lachlan Albemarl had put his hands. I was leaning breathless against the trunk of the poinciana, and my lips were smarting where he had kissed them, then smeared them with mercurochrome to heal the breach. Vermilion faced, a clown, I was so limp where I leaned that the flow of the tree in the wind took me on and we swayed together in the eddying red. The wind meant rain was coming.

Soon the red tears were joined by liquid tears, and the squall hit hard. Now that Lachlan Albemarl had gone I was not sure if I would be able to get myself home. I was cowering there in the red storm because I didn't know if I'd ever get out of it.

Finally I did come running down the slushing back of the road, which coiled me home. No use in it though, because Con had gone surfing, and Morgan was busy.

Morgan had her head shrouded in a black scarf, and she was reading a heavy book with a leather cover spotted in mould. There was something smoking acridly in a pan on the stove. My small body stalled at the door was not enough to make her look up, but when she heard me hiccup from the helter-skelter run home her eyes flicked up and she saw me leaning there, watching her with enormous black eyes, hair stuck to my skull and the Raggedy Ann mouth gaping wide, frightened and threaded with panting. She let out a scream. I knew that she thought that I was a demon. It took her a few seconds to realise that it was only me, her little girl.

She smacked me when she did.

—You dreadful child. You hideous dreadful naughty child!

She pinched my face between thumb and forefinger, scrutinising. She dabbed at the vermilion stain with a moistened finger.

—This looks like mercurochrome. It is mercurochrome. Did you hurt your face?

—No.

—So why have you put mercurochrome on it?

—I didn't.

—Well who did then?

—At school. Boy . . . boys at school.

—Well you shouldn't have let them. You look a fright. You realise it's not going to come off? And look at this—it's all along your leg, right up to your skirt!

She lifted my skirt and smacked me again when she saw the spreading blotches on my knickers, streaking my thighs.

—Go into the laundry and wash these knickers out. Don't come out until they're clean.

I went to the laundry sink and began to scrub. An hour later, Morgan towered at the door.

—Has it come out?

—No.

—Now you'll know never to do this again. It won't come out, not ever. Remember that before you get involved with such nonsense another time. Okay?

—Yes.

—Hang them out to dry then.

That night Lachlan Albemarl would not let me sleep. He smothered my dreams and forced me into memory, that place where I had to come face to face with him. Over and over again I saw him in the deserted school toilets after school, his sponge mouth squeezing against my mouth as he practised—parts felt nice until he got his teeth and bit a little, just to see what would happen. It was thorns. You are gagged, so perhaps you know what it is like not to be able to make a sound? My voice behind the gag could not wriggle free, and even when he removed it I could not speak. There were cuts on my tongue—I could taste the blood.

He was powerful. He knew how to fold limbs back and forth so that your body was like a knot you couldn't untie. He told me we were going to play a new game. Can you see like I can, his arctic eyes in the half light, calmly rebuffing my fear? And hands enlarging huge command, coolly experimental? Perhaps you can imagine that when he had put them in every place they could scientifically go, he examined the red drops and the tear drops and he took out the mercurochrome and painted over them. He planted the interlopers, the parasitic, shocking vermilion flowers expanding runny petals into crevices of skin and obliterating their host. But would this help those wounds to heal?

—There, Lachlan said, now we can go home.

Lachlan didn't have to tell me to keep quiet about it. I knew that was part of the game.

At home, I assembled the dolls. I removed their clothes and laid them all down in a row. Their bodies were resilient, tinted ivory or pink. I compared my brown skinny legs with theirs. There was obviously no comparison between these or any other parts. I did not correspond to them. When I looked for the spiral serpent it wriggled out of my mind, and I coughed and wheezed because I was terrified that my voice was deserting me. The cuts on my tongue were stinging. Perhaps my tongue had sustained lasting damage. I tried to see into the dolls' mouths. None of them had tongues, I could tell that much. They were so haughtily aware of this that they pressed their lips together, evaded my eyes, and refused to utter so much as a word.

4 The Fall

I thought I'd never see Lachlan again after that day. We'd finished sixth class. The next year we were going to separate high schools. I was going to the girls' convent in town. He wouldn't be able to corner me any more at lunch or after school. It was a form of identity crisis, as well as a relief. I was used to being his familiar, and it was hard to imagine who I would be without him.

All summer I stayed home, dazed by the smell of hot jacaranda blossoms inviting rot where they lay on the grass. I often got up in the jacaranda tree to hide from Morgan.

That day I was up there, swaying in my purple web, weaving my secret spells and pretending I was Morgan (don't all daughters, however estranged from their mothers, long to replicate them in some way, if only in fantasy?).

I saw Morgan coming out of the back porch and heading for the forest. Stones flicked from her thongs as she walked down the red dirt road on her skinny pole legs, poised and a little off balance as if she was tight-rope-walking down the back of a snake which might whiplash around and bite her. I understood. The road was like that—red and winding and scaled with pebbles, sleeping there in the hot sun of the day. You knew that underneath, it was alive. I always wondered where it went on the dark nights without the moon. It probably slithered deep into the cave, which was Morgan's destination now.

Morgan walked straight to the heart-shaped hole in the forest where the road slid in like a secret. It was a cave the colour of dark jade, where the leaves meshed together to seal the edges and make it shadowy and cool. Morgan stood at the verge of it, paused for a long while as the tree weighed me in a prolonged absence of wind. The universe scrutinised us. We were suspended inside its eye. We were inside the envelope of a suddenly irrelevant world which had turned white and empty, the mere surround for me, in the violet hammock of the iris, enclosing Morgan on the brink of the pupil. Everything tending that way, focused on the malachite darkness of the centre.

And then Morgan was going inside. At the moment that she was swallowed up the silence broke and the cicadas down the bottom of the valley screamed. And then I remembered what Lachlan had told me about the cicadas.

I looked down the back of the red road snake and it rose up before me, weaving in the air. There was a silken susurration as it rolled itself up and across my mind. I reached into my throat and found the ball of sound and tossed it through the centre of the spiral. It went up and out of the net. In only a moment the cicadas had caught it, and we batted it from valley to tree to hill, frenetically, until they narrowed to the pitch, their voices clustering closer and closer to it, hemming it in, banking up against it and finally smothering it so that the world, drained of colour, hung bleached on the hysterical line of sound. For a long time.

Then there was Morgan again, issuing monochrome from the tunnel, her clothes soaked, as mad as she'd ever been. Running straight down the road, she spotted me strung up in the tree with my mouth just a little open and recognised the expression on my face. She knew what I was doing. Before I had even stopped the sound she was shaking the tree, and very soon I was falling out of it. Clinging to me as the tree let me go, the purple. It surged back into the world with all the other colours as the sound dropped out of air and released everything. The resilient technicolour world was rushing towards Morgan in her faded black singlet with her biceps bubbled with the shaking. She would have beat me except I landed hard on the pebbly patch of ground and left her standing there, to all intents and purposes alone. Because the eye, wide open with shock at this turn of events, had sucked me into it pupil and closed the lid.

I know that Morgan stood, her neck and arms glistening with yellow cicada piss in the midday sun. Her singlet and shorts steamed a little in the heat. Apart from the cicada piss, there was an overwhelming smell of hot jacaranda blossoms, squashed and rotting in the grass. Insensible, her idiot child pressed her face close into bruised violet. Nothing moved, until a breeze sidled between Morgan's knees. At the prompt, she turned and went inside to call the doctor.

When the eye blinked open it was night and I was in bed with a broken left foot and bruises everywhere. In the light from the hallway, I watched my blackened elbows flex and quiver, and heard Con and Morgan fighting. It was a whispered fight. Those sounded like moths flying into the fire, a stumbling and fluttering until someone hit a mark. Then you could hear the sizzle of it. When the fight was dire, there was even a strange singed smell too. The sleep bat flapped unevenly out of the darkness and swiped me before I smelt it, but I did hear the odd flitter of their ill-matched sparring.

—. . . misfated . . .

—No. No. Murderous and how can you . . .

—. . . coincidences only and that's . . .

—. . . doctor said she could have died.

—But you must see, she's not *good.*

—Any mother . . . child . . . unnatural!

—Sin comes back, don't you see?

And then, clearly, Death loves this child, Con. She was not meant for this world. She is our curse. Maybe not just our curse alone. I dread to think what she will do when she has grown up.

—Morgan, you're mad. Stark raving mad.

The sleep wing, sweeping down, wiped it all out. But the singed smell was in the air that night, because I could smell it in the morning, clinging to the sheets. When Morgan came in and sat down on the chair next to my bed, she brought a swirling gust of it with her.

She leaned over me as I watched, and I saw the gulfs in her stringy neck flexing as she swallowed in preparation for the attack. She had her harsh eyes on.

—Dim, she began.

I squirmed in the bed, but I couldn't turn over because of my dead leg. I longed to turn my back on her despite the risks but I knew from my experiments earlier that morning that moving the leg would make a rocket of pain go sky-high. So I lay still and faced up to her.

—Just one thing, Dim. I know you did it on purpose.

What? The cicadas? Falling? Breaking my foot? Not dying?

—And you won't get away with it.

I wondered what she had been doing in the cave. Perhaps the cicadas had interrupted something important. It was only an experiment—I hadn't meant anything by it.

—Playing with your voice like that. It's dishonest. You're turning into a troublemaker. It's tough bringing up a kid who wants to make trouble, and can't tell the difference between right and wrong.

She fixed me with the harsh eyes. They had soft striated mushroom undersides of fear when she finished, whispering.

—I saw. You remember that one from the other times, don't you? Dim, I saw death come for you when you fell from the tree. Do you remember?

I couldn't answer. Of course I remembered death

from the other times. More than once, I'd clearly looked into the face she was calling death, but I hadn't seen that face when I fell from the jacaranda tree. I was out cold. I saw nothing at all. But I believed her. I believed that death had stood over me, deliberated over me.

—You didn't see?

—I was out to it. I didn't see anything.

I think that was my last chance with Morgan. She had made up her mind that it was death which bound us together, and when I denied that link I lost the last thing which Morgan admitted as a bond. Her face crisped over, and she seemed to make up her mind. She said—I can't have you here. I've told your father. He's agreed that next year you'll board at school. You can come home in the holidays. Hopefully the nuns will know how to take the liar out of you, because I sure as hell don't.

She stood up in a cloud of singed odour and went out.

5 Dolly

True to her word, Morgan sent me to board at the convent school. While I was there with the nuns, I was God's doll. He kept me a child. This was because he liked to play with me.

People noticed, as I grew older, that there were not the usual changes. I saw them looking at me, looking at my angled face all eyes and bones, looking at my body chafing in my clothes, sizing up the gawky not female not male not adult not child not anything shape of me.

I knew I was alien. I didn't worry, because God played with me. Every day, he'd cup me in his hand and every now and then he would work my stiff limbs back and forth back and forth, rake his fingers through my flat hair and flick my eyelids up and down so that they would not thicken and set into my skull. That flickering feeling was exquisite; the world would bat to and fro in a liquid white haze and flirt with me. I could see heaven in the gaps.

I occupied my spare time outside lessons and homework with sporadic reading and obsessive prayer. Other students saw me haunting the library like a wraith with my demented eyes averted from all corners, and perhaps they knew of my night-time prowls in the garden where the demons waylaid and perverted me. I had the loudest nightmares of any of the boarders. I talked to no one, because I terrified most.

The nuns saw in me a look which they recognised, and which they knew they must expel from that place. Accordingly, they bundled me out into the world more and more frequently, in the hope that good works would still the strangeness which possessed me. More and more frequently, I was pressured into offering a humanity to others which I knew I did not possess. The madness coming on, coming on.

At seventeen I still kept a secret hoard of dolls under my bed, packed up tightly into an old carton. I still talked to them, but any love I had for them was sick. It was the love of despair. I was not equal to their challenge. I understood now that I couldn't ever compete with their supremely studied, flawless impotence.

The days when I summoned the spiral serpent were the days I needed to discuss my cracked being, the hunger which dwelt there like a clawed feral cat. I'd glimpse it there, notched ears the record of a thousand spats, and ribs slicing its sides with starvation. Some days the howl of its voice scratched against the air near my face and I could feel the bird blood smeared with feathers on my stretched lips.

I would confess my sins. I would bare myself, a bony fabrication, and a failure at that. Any fool could see that I wasn't the real thing, wasn't genuine somehow.

—I was born from a gut of glass. Barbarella, hear me now I'm telling you something important. I came here because of Morgan's desperate last attempt. Scientists and magicians grappled with my will *not* to exist. They made me do it. Their science was too great for little me.

—You were made, Dimity, in the same place as me. In the very same place. But something went wrong. Instead of plastic, instead of perfection, they gave you flesh. You got cheated. If you'd only had the presence of mind to insist on total fabrication, if you'd only rebelled against their sentimental drive to make you normal, if you'd only spoken up, exercised your will, insisted that you wanted to be a Frankenstein creation. But that's always been your mistake, hasn't it Dimity? A little Dim? That's you, isn't it? No self-assertion. That's how you lost your one chance at flawlessness, at incorruptibility.

—Yes you're right, you are right. You're always right. You have the certainty of polymers. Endless chains of the same thing linked immaculately together. You've got no reason to doubt anything—your own makeup is so . . . convincingly consistent. You are too . . . hard.

Barbarella inflated her improbable breasts and boasted, I've got this body for ever.

—Until someone throws you out. Someone ultimately will tire of you.

—No you won't.

—Maybe. Maybe I'll outgrow you.

—Sweetheart, take one look at yourself. You've done that already.

—From the outside. If you count the years up. But inside I'm cracked. That's why we talk. If I wasn't so broken, I'd be talking to other people. Not to dolls. Even living dolls, like you.

6 The Dream Became a Nightmare

You would know that this was going to happen. It has been coming inevitably, just as it is inevitable that a child, unless something intervenes, will grow up. I think you've seen the place where I came from now. I have shown you what it was like. I've shown you the valley, and I've shown you the dream I dreamed there.

That dream is not over yet, of course. But it intensified. It intensified and became a nightmare. Are you still listening? My tongue is working overtime to draw up all these things. It is for you to maintain silence, and to listen carefully. Then you'll understand how the nightmare found its wings, tested them, and then took flight. Ssh. It's like this.

I went home every holidays. Every time I went back to the forest, Morgan seemed more distant, more hectic and more obsessed. She disappeared into the rainforest for hours at a time. I could see that Con was worried about her. Fair enough—she definitely wasn't normal.

The last summer I went there, I saw a lyrebird for the second time. I found it lying in the forest. Its neck was savaged, ragged red. Its eyes were gelled over with death. The details in its scrolling varied tail were plucked loose, roughened into a sad trailing. I brought it back home, crying, to show Con. He took a deep breath when he saw it, shaking his head. I knew he was nauseous.

—Feral cats, Dimmy. They're as big as panthers in there, and there's no controlling them. They prowl around as if they own the forest, cleaning out native species. Some of these birds will be lucky to see their way through the next ten years if the cats keep it up.

He threw up.

I saw something else that summer. I still don't know what it was. I only know that walking in the forest I espied the stringy limbs of what looked to be my mother, saw them flash through the endless thicknesses of trees and vines and palms and ferns. I knew better than to close in on her. She'd never have tolerated that, now even less than before. But I stopped for a moment, squinting, and I can say that it was her. Yes. Through the mesh of all that life, pushing and webbing and climbing and feeling its way in that dim and smothering place, I saw Morgan somewhere else, writhing on the forest floor and moaning to the humid air. Who could say why she rolled there like that, her body beaded in red mud and stockinged in clinging leaf litter? Who could imagine why she would be lying there and crying like that, reaching out with arms laced in scratches and fingers dressed red with the same mud, her head crowned in moss, butting rocks and buttressed roots? Was she yelling for the demons to possess her?

She thinks perhaps that she is looking over the back of someone. See, that's a humped stone there, hulking over her, shouldering her where she hangs on, clenched fingers. And those are roots, twined with her. She scrapes her rutted ribs against a shield of bark, corrugated just like her. Like to like. Is she alone?

If Morgan was rucking up her body, buckling and ricocheting, her face indistinct but rhapsodic and twisted (that much is certain), that was surely up to her, and if Morgan had the mud-red flowers splotched all along those secret places, then only Morgan knew. It was not show and tell. Please leave it at this: it was so dark and there were so many shapes, all competing for my eye—for anyone's eye—that I couldn't see what was real and what was not, and the overall effect was of confusion, a dreadful confusion and chaos. I couldn't tell if Morgan was alone with her horrible fancies, or if those fancies were real.

But this isn't about Morgan. This is my story. It's all I can do to keep her in check. Suffice to say that I came running out of the forest for the last time.

At dinner Morgan refused to speak to me. I left the table, and I heard her telling Con that she had no need for the third any more, and that there was no place for a third in that house henceforth. He remonstrated with her, but she was terse. I heard her say, We'll burn for this. I'll burn for what I did. And you'll burn with me. It wasn't right.

—What wasn't right?

—What I did.

—Did?

—I'm speaking of the third. Don't play dumb with me. Don't play dumb just like she does. You know what

I'm talking about. We all know about the third. She can speak. Really she can. She'll tell on me. One day she'll tell on me and everyone will know.

—Know what, Morg?

—That I cheated.

Back at the convent, I dreamed an appalling dream. A nightmare. I dreamed that there was an enormous fire. A fire which razed the rainforest and danced a ring around our house there. In the main bedroom, my parents' four-poster bed was decked out as a funeral bier. On it, Con lay dead, black ribbons around him. And Morgan, wearing her widow's weeds, danced with the fire, a lunatic reel which she kept up until it grew so hot that she withdrew into the house. Lamenting, Morgan threw herself across Con's breast. Her ululations vibrated on the air, already corrugated with heatwave. Outside, the feral cats yowled as their fur caught fire. The fire consumed the house. As it burned, the soil heaved up into a giant volcanic peak, with the house inside its vortex. It spat and seethed and belched forth sparks and coals, cinders and smoke. With one last explosion, it blew itself to pieces, buried Morgan alive and woke me up.

Part Two

FREAK

1 The Future

It was Barbarella I heard that day when the freak show came to town. It was because of Barbarella that I left the convent just before I graduated from my final year there. More than that though. I left because that was written into the story, this story of my life which I am trying to tell you. This next part of the story explains how I escaped from the forest. I won't explain where I went, only what I learned and how I changed. That's really what this next part of the story is about. About the way I refined my talents, shared them with a wider audience, accustomed myself to my own virtuosity. For although I am cursed, in some things I have been a very great success. You must believe this. Really, you can't do otherwise, since all you know of me is what I present to you. I do as I choose, and you, you are the listener, no more and no less. So believe.

Perhaps if you could speak you would ask what happened in the forest after I left. Perhaps even now you are struggling with those stitches to pose such questions. You squeak through the net, insistent, curious. I admit that this question of the dream of my childhood is a pressing one. I have more to say about this but not now. Now we can leave Morgan behind, I can neglect her, I can let her rot there on the forest floor with all the other biodegradables, let her lie there trussed in vines and gagged in leaves, on her bed of impaling roots. Because I really did escape her. I really did set myself free. There were many months when Morgan did not rule me, when I had respite from the dream. I was mad, yes. But not as crazy as the daughter that she had reared.

I was even fool enough to think that the curse was over. When I reached eighteen years old I smiled at myself. I was happy because now no one could make me go back there. I was independent and an adult. Fortune would beam at me. The curse was left behind, wrapped in the forest. Secret, it decomposed.

But I was telling you about Barbarella. About the way that she egged me on and sent me into my next acrobatic flirtation with the queer shadow of my difficult destiny. It happened on the main street of the town where I went to school. I was loitering there, fresh from another botched attempt at compassion, when I saw the freak show trundling towards the showground in a series of utes, vans, trucks and caravans.

While I stared, one of the vans stopped and disgorged a man. He waved it on and moved across the road to the place where I was leaning up against the entrance to the Empyre Cafe, licking an ice-cream and waiting for the sense of failure to wear off. The woman the nuns had sent me to help had opened the door and looked at me once before telling me that I had the eyes of her dead husband and closing the door in my face. I wasn't sure how to explain this to Sister Frances. I knew she would understand about my eyes—she had seen them herself so she knew they were unsettling—but I wasn't sure what she would have expected me to do. I didn't think that running away was the correct response. It wasn't the response she was seeking to instil in me.

The man now walking towards me made these thoughts disperse like so much incense smoke. Something about him arrested me. This man had insolence stamped on every pore of his body. He had insolent flighty hands—I saw this when he waved the van on. And now as he walked past me into the cafe I noticed his insolent beady eyes as they gave me a dismissive once-over, and his insolent mouth curling at the edges like heated plastic, and his insolent aquiline beak of a nose raised in a deep snort before he spat, once, into the gutter. Then he passed me and entered the Empyre. Looking after him I watched his very beautiful (and insolent) buttocks recede into the dead atmosphere of stirring fans and stale grease and I heard Barbarella say, Yum.

I think it was the sheer insouciant arrogance of that man which captivated me. There was an extraordinary power and certainty in his vainglorious composure. For a terrified wastrel like myself, so harried by my imperfections that I spent a part of each day articulating them to myself and my dolls and shunning all other contact, he represented freedom. A wondrous exotic bird, he flitted across my horizon and showed me another world. Ego.

Barbarella whispered, Go after this one. You don't

get his sort much in towns like this. Go on, see where he's going. Quick, or you'll lose him.

So when he came out, eating chocolate, I followed him. And kept on following him for some time after that, ignoring him every time he told me to get lost, until I really did get lost. But that's the future. That first time I followed him I arrived at the showground, where the freaks were setting up.

The freaks were freaky. They were genuine. In this show, a dwarf was as normal as the next person. Women with a single eye or three breasts worked side by side with men with webbed hands and feet, who in turn competed for ring space with people with so much body hair they looked furred. The sideshows revealed individuals whose cheeks were scarred from the nightly incursions of skewers through the soft skin that lined them, still others whose entire bodies were tattooed or whose genitalia were pendulous from the kitchen appliances which swung from them during the shows. Somebody was spangled with hundreds of gold body piercings, which she augmented every night. Another had curved fanged teeth that looked like those of a tiger. There were Siamese twins, joined at the wrist. There were the usual giants and obese men and women. There was also a one-legged man who had amputated his own leg using fishing line which he had progressively tightened over several weeks, cutting off the circulation and finally severing it.

In all this dizzying detail I felt invisible. It was a new feeling. For so many months I had been the resident ghost and demon at the convent, and I was used to creating a stir. But here, no one noticed me. I became my very own kind of freak, a sort of invisible woman. Through the flurry of vehicles, tents, ropes and people, I slid unmarked, close to the trail of the insolent man.

He went into one of the tents. I didn't want to walk in there. Not yet. I wanted to get out of my school uniform first. I knew it wasn't appropriate seduction attire.

Behind me the man with the webbed feet and hands had finished filling his tank. It was an enormous glass aquarium, with the name *Human Fish* painted on the side in ornate italic script. I turned to see him lowering himself into it. He swam underwater, weaving from side to side. The light shone through the membranous skin between his fingers as he spread them to the wall of the tank and gaped at me through the logo, a net of hair aureoling his bubbling face. He was saying something. I had a quirk of fear—in some tiny place I remembered one like him, cupping me close in sleepybye land under the deep blue sea, embracing me down there and never letting me go, never back to land where Morgan and Con were waiting for the boat to return.

I had to look away, over my shoulder. I saw the insolent man come out of the tent. A woman accosted him. She had big hair, big hips, big heels, Hollywood makeup, a whip, and three breasts slung up bronzed and oiled like gourds in a latex tricup bra. She flicked the whip lightly around his ankle, and pulled him a little towards her with a fetching giggle. He was laughing too.

He put one hand in his pocket, and the other on her shoulder. It was like watching a movie. I could even hear them.

—Look after something for me, will you, Vera? he said.

—Sure, Tone, sure. In your pocket is it? Show me.

She reached for the front of his pants. At the same time, he took something out of his pocket and slipped it between two of her breasts.

—What is it, Tone?

He didn't answer her before she screamed. Stamping her feet, she put both her hands to her chest. Still laughing, the man strolled off, leaving her shrieking.

Standing out in the open, watching, I was isolated, still. Everyone else bustled around me, ignoring the woman's screams. I couldn't stop looking at her. Her eyes picked me out too. At once she came running towards me, squealing, Get this bloody thing out of my bra!

I looked down a giddying, heaving fault line sandwiching a desperate baby green tree snake, warping and writhing where she had it pinned with panic. She was hyperventilating. Beads of sweat sparkled all over her exposed chest and shoulders. The big hair, acrylic snap-frozen blonde on the top of her head, didn't move at all. False eyelashes clapped back and forth as I poked my hand quickly in, fished the snake out and shoved it in my pocket, resolving to keep it forever since it was his.

She clutched my shoulders.

—Is it gone?

—Yes.

—That bastard.

She lifted her arms and settled her bra, easing all three breasts into their places, then narrowed her eyes. The lashes scrunched together so thick they looked like two brooms seen from below.

—I'm going to get him for that one.

Turning, she strutted off, her buttocks grinding against her g-string. There was a puff of powdery dirt every time she planted her platform thigh boots on the roughed-up turf of the showground.

A splurting surfacing noise and Human Fish's head appeared over the edge of the tank. He burst out in a burbling liquid laugh.

—Show in itself, isn't it?

—Yeah.

—You in the company?

—No.

—Why not? Nothing to show?

—No.

—Nothing? There's *nothing* freaky about you?

Before I'd even considered the question, I'd answered him from a frank space totally separate from my crippling shyness. The answer surprised me.

—There's plenty freaky. I just don't know if it's showable, if you know what I mean.

—Darl, it's always *showable.*

He dipped his head underwater again, and shook it out in the air in a gyrating dazzle of drops.

—Excuse me, but who was that?

—That was Vera Amorphous.

—And the man?

—That was Antonio Houdini Grieg.

The snake wriggled in my pocket, making my legs tingle. I could feel my life changing, right then and there. I thought it was because I knew his name. But Human Fish knew better.

—The future's coming for you. You've got that look. Go and see Claudia.

—Who's Claudia?

—Madame Futura. That's her caravan down there. See?

He pointed with his interconnected fingers. They were already starting to whorl up from the water.

—Go on. If you're early she might not charge you.

Barbarella niggled at me, Go on. Maybe something good's going to happen to you. We both know it's unlikely. But you'll never know if you don't ask. Best to be prepared. Maybe then you'll maximise your chances of grabbing onto any shred of luck that comes your way. Remember what Sister Dom says: forewarned is forearmed.

Human Fish had plunged back down to the bottom of the tank, and sat there, fanning his limbs back and forth. He waved me goodbye with both hands as I walked back down the alley of tents, towards the purple and gold caravan where Madame Futura hulked over her crystal ball, humming old love songs with a too-much-jewellery tinkle of bangles, earrings, necklaces and anklets, the air thick with incense. She welcomed me inside with a beaming grin.

—Well then, early bird, it looks as if you have the worm!

She pointed to my pocket, where the tree snake was oozing forth in a muscled emerald trickle. I scooped it up and pushed it back into my dress. I felt nervous. The future was a big place and I didn't want to get lost there like I had in the past.

—Sit down. You want a reading?

—Yes.

—Here, give us your hand.

I held my palm out.

—Not the left, darlin, the right one.

I swapped them and waited.

—Well then! You are shortly to travel. Your path crosses ours for a while, and then it breaks off. Perhaps you'll join. You have something to show?

—No.

—But surely. There are marks here, marks that tell you are out of the ordinary. It is this spiral here, coiled around just like the snake in your pocket. You see this one? This is the place where you are not ordinary. Something to do with the neck, the throat . . . ?

—The spiral serpent.

—Sorry, darlin'?

—My voice. I can transfer my voice.

—Show me.

I put Antonio Houdini Grieg's voice over in the corner.

Madame recognised it at once and let off a firework of a laugh.

—Well then! A ventriloquist! We don't have one of those here now. We used to, but that was more than a decade ago. That's your in. No reason why you can't get up on a stage and do that for an audience. They'll love it, with the right props and some stage direction. I'll take you over to Mr Wu tomorrow morning if you like and he'll audition you.

I stared.

—Honey, it's written there on your hand. You don't go against that stuff—it only wastes time.

—What happens to me if I join the show?

—You want the full reading you'll have to wait while I rev up the crystal.

She fixed her eyes on the crystal. In the shrouded light of the caravan it glowed amethyst from within. I had never seen anything so beautiful. I was so mesmerised by it that I started when Madame began to speak in a sonorous voice, her glazed eyes still focused on the crystal.

—Like the cat, you walk by yourself. Your destiny is to be alone. Like the cat, you are the witch's familiar. Take great care, for this part of your destiny is the darkest, and it is drinking black mist into my crystal even now as I try to look for it. Watch when you dissemble, because the malice will find you. Again like the cat, you will have nine lives, one for each year it took to make you, and you will die eight times and be renewed. You will die once by water, once by snake-bite, twice by a fall. But the cat always falls on its feet, and you will survive. You die once by starvation, once by poison. And you die three times by fire. The very last time that you die, it is the fire that takes you out of this life, to the fire that awaits you in the next.

There was a long pause, then Madame looked up and shook her head, smiling a little groggily.

—So, she resumed brightly, what did I tell you?

—You told me I had nine lives, like the cat.

—Well fancy! Something in your eyes, love. Aloof, a bit hungry maybe. Like a cat, a bit.

The next day I auditioned and was accepted into the freak show. They were leaving in a week's time. At the end of the week, I got my carton of dolls from the convent and left town. I never went back to that place again. And I never saw Morgan and Con again, except in my vivid and torturing dreams. The last words I heard in that town were Barbarella's. She'd already picked up some choice phrases from all the new people she was mixing with.

—Come on Dimity, let's get the fuck out of this dump.

Antonio Houdini Grieg wouldn't let me near him. The whole show knew it. They watched me trot after him, besotted, all day and all night. When I wasn't on the stage or in bed I was at his ankles like a blue heeler gone wrong. The kind ones tried to warn me off him. Like SadoMan.

—Dimmy, he said one night as he sharpened his daggers against the whetstone, you'd best leave Tone alone.

—Why?

—He's no good for you, love.

I looked away, got an eyeful of Vera Amorphous as she moved past me, shoulders flung back, one slack arm gracefully raised over her head, her breasts shuddering skyward in her spangled bikini top. Well lubricated in baby oil and fake tan, her mature stretchmarked belly pouted rhythmically where it rolled sinuously over the waistband of her fluorescent orange harem pants as she practised swallowing coins with her navel, introducing them one by one at her cleavage and contriving their descent by way of her remarkable muscle tone.

—Dimmy, listen to me. That one's a heartbreaker. It'll be the worst thing for you if he takes up on the offer. God knows it's plain enough what you're after, kiddo, but look elsewhere. The selection may be a bit limited in a hellhole like this, but . . .

—What I'm after?

—Dimmy, sweetheart, it's as clear as mud that you want to get laid.

—Laid?

He sighed in exasperation, then pulled out his skewers, freshly sharpened and disinfected, from the red velvet cloth in which he'd swaddled them fifteen minutes before. He held them up in the light, and they gleamed viciously.

—See these?

—Yes.

—You've watched me poke these through my cheeks in my act, haven't you?

—Yes.

—Here, count them. How many do you get?

—Fourteen.

—One for every young kid's bubble he's burst. They fall for him, he fucks them, then the whole thing blows up in their faces, sure as if he'd poked one of these into it. Dimmy, don't join the bloody queue, okay?

—But . . .

—But you love him, but you need him, but you can change him, but this time it'll be different, but fucken nothing, kiddo. That's what they all say. Next thing I'm ruining one of my best knives trying to scrape the goddam mess off the floor. Read my lips now: KEEP AWAY. You go after him, sweetie, and you're a masochist. I'm sure your mum told you that's not healthy.

I didn't know what I wanted from Antonio Houdini Grieg. I just knew I wanted it. I was a seventeen year old weirdo kid fresh out of a convent school and what I knew about relationships could have been written out on the point of one of SadoMan's skewers, with room to spare. But I knew that the insolence which Antonio Houdini Grieg peppered into every word, expression and action was infinitely desirable, and that I had to offer myself up to it. I realised that this was not going to be easy, and I tried just about everything. Without success.

I'd found him, the first morning after I joined. He was standing next to the river at dawn, smoking. He was elegant in a pair of King Gee shorts. In the sultry northern weather he wore no shirt. I was wearing the only clothes I had—the fawn coloured t-shirt and shorts which I'd brought from the convent, and a pair of thongs. It was better than a school uniform. I went up to him.

—Hi.

He regarded me for a moment before replying.

—Good morning.

—I have something of yours.

His raised eyebrows clearly suggested that this seemed very unlikely.

So I reached into the pocket of my shorts and brought out the tree snake. In the few days I'd had it, it had already grown a few centimetres.

—I've been feeding it on small frogs and beetles.

I smiled tentatively.

His lip curled slightly.

—That's not mine.

—But . . .

—I found that in my tent and got rid of it. I don't want it back.

—But . . .

—See ya.

It looked as if the snake, if it belonged to anyone, belonged to me. Antonio Houdini Grieg had turned around and walked off. The mist rose off the river like the ghosts of Con and Morgan. As usual, my social success was in extreme jeopardy.

2 I Bruise My Heel

I'd been with the freak show for what felt like forever. My old life had receded completely. I couldn't imagine being the person I had been or doing the things I had once done, though I knew that that person lived on inside me, and those things had formed me.

I got up on stage every night. Isolated in the middle of that space, singled out by the lighting, I confronted my fantasies and my fears, the same ones that were left over from that old life. That was what made the show work. There was enough real stuff to engage the crowd. I performed shrouded in a white dress, a ghost of Con and Morgan's crazy child, dancing up there with a painted face and strung-out hair full of oil. I sat up on my chair with BabyLove on my knee and had her tell me all her secrets.

There was a cluttered black textural void ahead of me every night. That was the audience—darkness netting titters and whispers, body odour, food aromas and perfume, the crunch of teeth on toffee apples. It surged against the island where I lived with the dolls. To keep it at bay, I summoned the serpent and banked my voice up at the edges of the stage like sandbags. Sometimes when I was daring I threw it right out into the black tumult of the sea, hoping it would swim back to me without getting laced up in the net. It managed this feat every time—glossy as a dolphin it would weave a true path through the chaos and flip itself back onto the dry land of my island.

Except one night when someone from the sea hitched a lift and ended up beached on the periphery of my world.

—Dim. Dim, it's me.

Who was it? Was it death, coming back for a visit? It must have been because there was a hand clutching me, and it had reached right for my vulnerable place, my left heel.

The lights had dimmed and the show was over. The tide was ebbing, the ebony sea sucking through the door of the tent and out into the big open night which awaited it. But it had left me this one piece of flotsam jetsam, which had got its hooks into my foot.

—Don't you remember me?

—Let go of my foot.

—I remember you, Dim. I remember you sitting under the poinciana tree at school, the first girl I ever kissed. Even with that makeup on, I can tell it's you. What the hell are you doing here?

I was afraid that he would pull me off the island and down into the pit, now emptied of ocean, where he dwelt alone. I wanted him to let go of my heel. If this was not death it might just as easily be the devil.

—Don't you remember me, Dim? I'm Lachlan, Lachlan Albemarl. See, here's my card.

He handed me a card.

—You know I could get you out of this joint, get you into bigger and better things. A bit of help from me and you could really make it. You've got the basics; I could give you the rest. Why don't you come and see me one day and discuss it? You're wasted in a dump like this.

I watched him, holding the card. His hand was massaging my foot. I remembered him, and knew his potency.

—Cat got your tongue, Dim?

A woman came up behind him. She was a lifesize version of Barbarella. Except for her eyes—instead of glassy cupidity she had mooneyes, luminous with waxing-waning instability, shreds of emotion straying over them like cloud. She slid both hands around his waist and peeked at me from over his shoulder. I could see that she was appalled by my face, masked with makeup but still radiating fear.

—Time to go, honey, she said, her hands smoothing his shirt.

I think she saved me. I trembled there at the maw until she intervened, and my foot flexed free of the hooks.

—Nice to see you again Dim, he was murmuring. Don't forget what I told you eh?

It was a narrow escape.

That night I got drunk with SadoMan and TatMax after the show. It was the first time I'd ever been drunk. We'd gone back to TatMax's tent and SadoMan asked

Tats to tattoo him. He wanted a remembrance of his daughter, Annelise Rosa, who'd been abducted by her mother's family at the age of four, and taken to a new life in New Zealand. She'd be six now. Tats had already mapped the design out on SadoMan's left buttock. It was a beautiful design of a sun rising over Annelise Rosa's name, in small clean letters.

—So that the sun will always shine on her in that far off Land of the Long White Cloud, SadoMan kept repeating, maudlin.

Tats was humming. The designs around his lips contracted as he pursed them to make the sound. There were jungles of creatures and plants and ideas roiling on his arms as he filled in the design.

SadoMan, who was pretty drunk, was asking when Tats was starting.

—Hurry up, mate, we haven't got all night.

Tats winked. His eye was swallowed up by the phoenix which nested below it. He'd finished.

—I want one too.

—No, Dimmy, SadoMan protested—you don't need to do that to yourself.

—No, I do.

—Why?

—I need protection.

—From what?

—See this left heel?

—Yeah. What about it?

—I broke this heel once. Another time it got bit by a snake. Both times I nearly died. This heel is my weak place, and it needs a lucky charm. Tats, can you do one there that looks like this?

I drew it on the notepad SadoMan had used to work out his design.

—What's that—a spiral?

—The spiral serpent.

—Eh?

—It's my totem animal in the place I come from.

Tats was sold on the idea.

—That'll look fantastic, just wrapped around the heel of your foot. Here, come up on the table and lie on your tummy.

—Dimmy, love, are you sure you want to go through with this? What'll your parents think?

—My parents are dead.

—O Lord. Poor baby with no daddy, like my poor Annelise Rosa.

The tattoo was completed with SadoMan sobbing in the corner. He never could hold his liquor.

The spiralling curve of my tattoo was etched very lightly with tiny spars, like the little hooks of the wait-a-while tree. It was the most stunningly simple tattoo which TatMax had ever done, and he was inordinately proud of it. Though utterly patterned himself, he had respect for subtlety.

—And do you know what? Barbarella exclaimed. It didn't even hurt!

I could only see my tattoo from a few positions. The easiest was when I balanced on my right leg, bent my left leg backwards and looked over my left shoulder. Whenever I felt fatigued or underconfident, or sensed any type of threat, I would shrug off my sandal, take up this position and look down on the beautiful tight whorl of my power, concentrated there on my heel.

The tattoo was as delicate as a tracery, a fluid engraving which was more than skin deep. It soaked into the skin. This was its protection and its magic. It was the power of the snake which had bitten me there, a reminder of the gift the snake had passed on to me along with the poison, a token of the talent which death had bequeathed me when I was given up once more to life.

In the evenings before the show I would catch insects and other things to feed the tree snake, which I was keeping in a basket in my tent, under my bed with the dolls. Then I would lie down on my mattress, extending my left leg over my head, and stare fixedly at my tattoo, drawing on it for the performance.

Once Antonio Houdini Grieg walked in when I was doing this. Mr Wu had asked him to tell me that I was on early. He came grudgingly, muttering along the way about the stupid crawling kid and her silly schoolgirl crushes and the unrecognised value of his precious time in that ridiculous place.

He opened the flap of the tent without knocking, stared when he saw me lying there with one leg poised in air, meditating.

—What on earth are you doing?

—Looking at my tattoo, I replied breathlessly. Want to see?

He grunted. I lifted my heel higher, trembling all over, terribly excited to be revealing this precious emblem to him, the man I loved. A part of me was sure that this would seduce him. Even if I couldn't make him notice me, I could surely make him aware of my potency through the wondrous patterning of this very powerful design. It was a dizzying fantasy, a fantasy that he would look on this tattoo and fall hopelessly for me, drop into my lap like a heavenly gift, plummet, enchanted, delirious, overcome, straight to my waiting embrace.

—I think tattoos look slutty on girls. What is it anyway—a scribble? You'd better shut your legs and get off that bed, Wu wants you on early. That's what I came to tell you.

He sneered at my tattoo so hard that I could almost feel it curling up tighter to protect itself from the force of his scorn.

3 Into the Flower

I decided finally that the only way to get to Antonio Houdini Grieg was to get on the same level as him. That meant overcoming one of my most dominant fears: my fear of heights. Because going to his turf meant going right up in the air, right up into the top of the show tent to the network of ropes which webbed it. It was up there that Antonio lived and breathed. Like a swallow he dipped and swung in the air above the crowd. He was a trapeze artist. In the freak show he was a rarity, a bit of light relief. For each of us had some human curiosity, some exploited flaw, bizarre or meaningless talent, a genetic kink to flaunt, and in some cases a deformity. Alternatively, there was a living to be made from bloodymindedness—a psychological warp which bred fascinating brutalities performed upon the self or accomplices, experiments or rituals which held a bug-eyed crowd in thrall. Morgan would have been a raving success here, if she'd worked up a suitable act.

In this world of gargoyles, Antonio Houdini Grieg was an angel. Dancer, athlete, he dangled his beautiful and insolent body before people like a bauble on a string, a lovely toy withheld, a technicolour human yoyo that was always out of reach. He had trained the insolence, honed it to this point of arrogant temptation and refusal, and made it his career.

In that whole company, he was the only one who had true star quality and talent, rather than the mutant fascination born of some twisted feature, proclivity or ability. As you can see, he was by no means a freak, unless you could count his insolence, which *was* unnatural.

It stood to reason. I could sit down there on the ground watching him practise or perform, like a cat watches a teasing pendulum swing just out of its reach. Or I could screw up my courage, shattered after that fall from the jacaranda tree all those years ago, and go up there to the eyrie where he flitted and perched and plumed himself, shitting on the plebs below.

So, hardened by his disdainful glances and his insouciant refusals, I prepared myself that night to climb up the place where he practised in the beam of just one weak light. It was four in the morning, and everyone else was in bed. Perhaps he couldn't sleep, because he was still up there (SadoMan had implied that Antonio had hideous dreams, the retributive action no doubt of his higher-self rebuking his dastardly lower-self). He was frowning, I could make that out from below as I put my first tentative fingers around the rope ladder and began to skin up it.

He saw me coming, wobbly uncertain ungrounded, gripping the rope hard as I reached the platform to see him, a fluid arc sweeping across the tent, silhouetted one brief instant against the faint light of the bulb on the other side, to land nimbly on the platform over there. The swing, released from the supple grip of his long-fingered hands, inscribed a looser, more extended shuddering arc as it bore its message of insolent challenge back to me. I rose to it, caught it, trusted to a swell of tiny biceps as my feet trod new on air and I was borne in a gust of panic and resolution across the distant ochre sandpit of the floor straight towards him and smack into him because he was so surprised I'd done it that he couldn't even move aside.

Our two souls, colliding up in mid-air in a cloud of hope and insolence: mine clinging, entwining, hungry, and his rebutting, loathing but yet in some part won over (perhaps by my courage?) because he held me as he'd caught me, hips packed in splat! to his, legs coiled around his muscled thighs, arms wrapping his neck, one big hand on my bum, and his other steadying the whole unlikely combination against the rope rails of the platform. Both of us, sweating and panting, in a tangle of swing.

He gave me a look of astonished disgust, then relinquished his hold on the rope rail and sat down, with me in his lap, just like the doll I wanted to be.

—You are one crazy bitch, he finally told me.

—I love you.

—Yeah, a bitch on heat. You've followed me for yonks, hanging out for it. And now this—it beats everything. You could have got killed, or killed *me* with your amateur fooling.

His hand on my back, holding me there like I

sometimes held my dolls in my act, supported me as the other went for the buttons, the secrets, the hunger. He bit my neck and my ear, hard, and tipped me down on the platform.

—So you'll get it, okay? You'll get what you want.

While I was getting it I couldn't really gauge whether it was what I had wanted at all. I was still asking myself when he picked me up and sat me on the narrow band of the trapeze, legs out stray and hair in my face, limp as a rag doll with a big silly doting smile, flushed red cheeks and blank eyes, my scrawny tush hanging over the sheer drop grinning to receive it, waiting for the love wave to hit me.

—Okay, so you got what you wanted. How's it feel, Dim?

I opened my mouth, but I couldn't think what to tell him. I was wishing he'd kiss and cuddle me and run his fingers through my hair, like I'd seen others do. I didn't think I could tell him that. I still wasn't scared, watching his perfect elongated fingers flex their hold on the swing where he had me poised, precarious again in air.

—In the Kama Sutra they do it on swings, Dim. Would you like that, eh? How would you like that?

—I . . .

And then he let go, at the same time giving me a big push, and because I wasn't expecting it, wasn't even holding on where my limp fingers curled around the ropes of the swing, I sailed through space in the swing's arc only so long before my weight, slight as it was, propelled me out of it and I flew still further, supported only by air, in one long slow-motion flourish before I plummeted breathless down, clipping the edge of the safety net in a sickening slap and squash of rag doll body before I came to ground. The last thing I heard as I whistled out of the ether was Antonio Houdini Grieg saying, Shit.

SadoMan told me, when I woke up out of the coma nine days later, that he'd found me at dawn, splayed out on the floor with my dress up like a parachute (ineffectual). Just my lean body like a twig discarded from the canopy above, bent and floppy against the ochre grain of the sand. No sign of anyone else. And up on the right platform, some blood, but none in the ring. The safety net hadn't caught me, but it had broken my fall, and in a back-handed kind of way I owed it my life.

True to my life's training in subterfuge, I didn't tell him what really happened.

—Dimmy, what were you doing up there, mate?

—I was practising.

—Practising what?

—I . . . I wanted to learn to fly.

—Like Tone?

—Yeah. I thought if I could learn, he might notice me. Maybe love me, if I knew how to exist in his element, up in the air.

—Dimmy, what did I tell you?

I counted the scabs on his stigmatised hands and

avoided the solicitous gaze which he was administering from his gentle sadomasochist's heart.

—Dimmy, no use ignoring me. I told you to steer clear of that stuck-up fool. He's a nasty piece of work. Now what really did happen up there?

I moved on to counting the scars along his right arm, delicate hairline wisps which spattered it and occasionally crisscrossed. I was up to twenty-three, counting the crossed ones as two each, before he rummaged for a moment in a back pocket and thrust a screwed-up bundle under my nose. I looked up at him.

—What's this?

—Your knickers, kid. They were up on the platform.

He stood up, dropping them in my lap. He clumped to the door of the caravan, shutting it behind him. I knew he knew I was lying.

There was something else which I concealed. I concealed it from you, you poor mute blind audience who doesn't know any better. But I'm coming clean, because I want to tell the truth in this story of mine. So much is performance, lies, nightmare, artifice or knowhow that I have to try wherever I can to tell everything in its plainest way. When I was up on the platform underneath Antonio Houdini Grieg, all I could see were the flowers, rending red and covering the whole quilted draping roof of the tent, obliterating even the sweating beaky face of Antonio Houdini Grieg as it glared into mine. The whole world for those few seconds was flowers. Now you know.

The next day they let me up. I had no broken bones. I sat with Madame Futura in her tent and drank jasmine tea.

—Well then darlin', didn't take you long to use up one more of those lives of yours, did it?

I put my nose into the tea cup and breathed deep. Death was no stranger to me, and life was something that had been forced onto me anyway. The fact that death and I had held hands that night was just one more intimate contact with an old friend. Nothing out of the ordinary.

Madame Futura winked—You gonna leave that silly primping rooster alone now, love?

—Madame, I can't, for I love him.

—Darlin', when love comes your way you'll know it by the look in his eyes. A man that looks at you with self pride, whose every waking moment is evidence that he thinks he's better than every other creature on this good earth; that man's not gonna give you any love worth having. You may be having the falls now darlin' but that's where he's headed in the end, the day'll come when the devil whips the swing out from under his tightassed pride and that'll be the end of him. Mark my words. No need for crystal ball gazing to suss that one out.

She glanced into the crystal, and her brow crinkled up.

—What is it Madame?

—Nothing love, nothing. Time you went and I got ready—I'm on tonight.

When I went back to my tent, I pulled the box out from under the bed, unveiled Barbarella and called up the spiral serpent.

—Barbarella, I'm in love.

—Yeah, no wonder. He's a dish. So what are you doing about it?

—I'm in pursuit.

—And is it working?

—Yes. Before I fell, we . . . he . . .

—Okay, so he loves you.

—You reckon?

—Of course. That's what happens. When it's love, that's what happens.

—So I should keep going?

—Of course.

—But he never came to see me while I was in recovery.

—He probably couldn't stand to see you reduced to that.

—No. No he probably couldn't. What should I do now? Should I wait until he comes to find me or should I go looking for him?

—Take the initiative for a change. Stop being so passive. Someone else'll get him if you don't, a hot number like him. No, you've got to go after him, and there's no time like the present, Dimity, you stupid girl. Go out there and look for him. You're a tiger, okay? A temptress. Go and stalk him, track him down. That's what he's waiting for.

So I got cleaned up and went outside. It wasn't long

before I found Antonio Houdini Grieg, just finished his performance and still wearing his sequined shorts. I decided to do just as Barbarella said, to follow her excellent advice and stalk my quarry, pick my moment for approaching him. He had crossed the whole show before he reached his destination, with me slinking in the shadows behind him.

It was inside the convulsed tent of Vera Amorphous that I saw the golden fake tan bum of Antonio Houdini Grieg finally slip with a jungly flash of green sequins.

I followed him in. Like a butterfly I was fluttering at the door and readying myself for the foray into sweet that I could smell. I prophesied the most sugared fragrant glutinous fluid experience cupped just out of reach—shall I shan't I shall I shan't I, until my flickering disclosed beyond the lip of the tent the red satin petalled well of Vera's bed and the stretched-out wavering praying mantis limbs of Antonio in a predator's dance before a predator twice his size and more dangerous: that incautious arrogant dandy dangling his wanton g-string above the noses of Vera and Camera Lucida, sprawled together at a crimson heart of mussed up sheets. Their hungry mouths gaped and moued, and their crooked arms reached for him.

I didn't stop to think about what I was doing. I was so anxious, so stricken with desire and care for his safety that I rushed right in to pull him from those paired peaked lips which sure enough would have swallowed him if I had not intervened—can you imagine my shock when he turned upon me naked and beautiful having shed his limey skin and told me to piss off?

Vera and Camera had laughter visible in those mouths! It was solid stuff, their laughter. Solid and invincible stuff. They put their supplicant hands together and Vera pleaded, Please Dim, leave him alone.

—Buzz off now, love, Camera advised with another block of laughter wedged under her tongue (wouldn't melt in her mouth).

I hovered, translucent, at the flap. When Antonio joined in the laughter I edged backwards and was gone.

I couldn't see any more for tears. I found my way by sonar sobs to Madame Futura's caravan, hoping that she would be back from being cut in two and that she'd be able to put me together again. But the caravan was empty. Nowhere to go so I slid the bolt across the door, sat down on the purple plush divan and hunched myself over Madame's crystal ball. I couldn't see tomorrow in it, only my own face, which sorrow had stripped pale. How could I have a future anyway? I was sure that my life would end now that Antonio Houdini Grieg didn't love me.

And that is just what happened.

Inside the caravan, I was safe from outside. It was tight and dark and stuffy. Every now and then, a pulse went through as someone brushed past outside and nudged the shell. The elephants lunged with trunks like coiled lassos slapped ears tail hairy haunch against the side of my world, loose children whined and clung there with sticky floss fingers while roadies with thuds and groans manoeuvred heavy objects around me. The rocking lulled me and I fell into an exhausted doze.

While I was asleep she came to me. Morrigan, my demon mother, trailing a black shroud. She knew I had been slighted, and she was determined that I should have my revenge. Her beautiful black eyes, floating liquid in the cavern of her wise face, winked three times, and she told me that this world would end in hellfire and damnation. This was my fate, but also my responsibility.

When the next thing happened, I still was asleep. I did not do what I did in a waking state. This was no action for awareness; it was the fruit of a desire which had glossy leaching roots in the dark dream world and couldn't stand the light of consciousness. But it was a desire so strong, so commanding, that it could govern a sleeping body, and make that body do its bidding. A desire much much stronger than my desire for Antonio Houdini Grieg. So when I stood up and unbolted the door, my breath yinyang-balanced in my lungs smooth and even, no ripple of trouble, my eyes were closed. I walked blind.

This is my excuse. Or my fantasy. It is the truth too, since these are one and the same. How else could I have lifted that immense orb, Madame Futura's beachball-sized crystal, unless I was possessed? As if I, with my slender frail limbs, could take on the swollen stony potential of the future single-handed, and launch it at the world!

Because that is what I did. Holding Madame Futura's most precious asset close to my belly, my feet glided sure over the runged steps of the caravan, and I moved through the milling crowd. It is true that SadoMan, sitting on the steps of the caravan adjacent to Madame's and contemplatively rubbing salve into his wounds, snickered.

—Preggers, are you, Dimmy?

And it's true that I answered him.

—Yeah Sado, I'm just about to bring the future into the world.

I also confirm that I came to the flap of Vera Amorphous's tent for the second time that night, and sent my voice in once to probe that hot cave and check that the quarry was within.

—Antonio honey?

—Yeah, Camera baby?

—That wasn't me, Ants.

—Sure it was sweetheart, don't get twee with me—it sure as hell wasn't Vera, was it Vera?

—No, honey.

—But . . .

—Look, you attention-seeking bimbo, will you just . . .

—Dim, what the hell are you doing—playing mothers and fathers or something didn't I tell you to . . .

And then the future sailed through the air like a huge block of ice and not only knocked Antonio out cold, opening his head like an eggshell, but smashed the gas lantern into the sullied blossom of Vera's blood-red bed and started the great conflagration which closed the freak show forever.

But before that happened, I woke up. Woke up to

see the cupped brain of Antonio and the two praying mantises writhing and squealing in the burning flower, their appalled anger and fear an astonishing vortex which they pulled me into.

In there was a dire smell of all of our hair burning along with synthetic costume asphyxiating me—no that was Camera who had her meaty fingers around my neck caressing it slow tight strangling like wringing towels and the ringing kept going right into my ears and chimed along with the fire alarm while Camera's one blue eye with the turquoise shadow on the lid was a skewer through the centre of my forehead and Vera had clawed my breasts until they were red too like the bed but she'd passed out now must be smoke inhalation even Camera's grip was loosening and she was tumbling back supine deep into the flower cup black around the edges now as she languorous no anger any more spread her tubular legs and sighed mmmmmmmmmm into the heated oblivion she let it in and was abandoned

Fainted too for a moment I rested there with my cracked lips just parted against Vera's crisping third nipple sapped and ready for nothing to come to me like it had to them because why should I survive when they had succumbed since I was a murderer if not also guilty of arson but there was another desire in me, and that was even stronger perhaps than the desire which had been at the helm when I created myself as a murderer, and it was the desire to live, which unfurled itself into the acrid air, and saved me just as I gave myself up to death.

And that's how I was born into the world one more

time. I came naked, with a globed head wet with tears and blood. My tender skin was ridged and seamed by fire. Curled on the ground twenty metres away from the inferno which engulfed the main tent, all the caravans, and most of my colleagues at the freak show, I breathed yinyang again.

My latest meeting with death had not robbed me of everything. Though I had no eyelashes and no hair, I had been born with property. I came into the world coiled around a huge crystal, as big as a beach ball.

I sold Madame's spectacular deep indigo crystal to one of the tinpot operators who descended on the town after the fire. In death, that petty and inglorious little cavalcade had verily become a media circus, and there were astonished whispers about the high prices which these souvenirists would pay for memorabilia. From my refuge in the bush which fringed the town showground, I had seen them scavenging through the site during the first days after the accident, turning over the blackened embers in search of our miserable bric-à-brac. I watched them set up stalls, saw them haggling over the charred remnants of the freak show, wheeling and dealing in the detritus from all those poor wasted lives. Hungry and with weeping wounds I took stock of my only asset, and approached one of the stalls, rolling the crystal painstakingly before me over the field of ash and cinders. A clogged silence fell like a curtain over the squabbling merchants and their customers. Everyone watched as laboriously, every action an agony, I reached the nearest stall. The woman who did the deal could barely look at me, she was so shocked and disgusted by my disfigurements. I was past caring. I needed the money to get to the city. I felt guilty but what use was the crystal to poor Madame Futura now?

The fire damaged me unbearably, sent me to my dissolution. My companions, the dolls and the tree serpent, had perished, leaving me fragmented, wild, scarred and very sick. I became the doll containing all the others. An eggshell cupped around a dense competition of voices. Because curiously, the dolls, whilst destroyed, had come inside. Wax-faced and ill, I hardly noticed that I was now so skilled that I could project my voice without their physicality as my focus. I didn't even take note that my skills had been so honed by performance that I could do any voice, any time.

Because I was desperate, my talent went silent. As if once more I was mute, unable to reach my own powers. Frightened, I asked myself if Morgan's curse had found me again. I suffered terrible anxieties thinking that I would lose my voice altogether, and be as silent as I was in my early childhood. The only thing that reassured me was my tattoo, still cleanly etched on my heel, undamaged by the fire. Even though I couldn't attempt to exercise my power, this marking gave me the only signal that I still had it, and provided a form of amulet against the further depredations of the curse.

So my voice was given over to other more trivial games, and for a while I did not put the spiral serpent into play. Until suddenly I found something worth playing for: another voice. And in a rash of lives used up I cast myself on the wheel of a fast-spinning present and bet my body in another desperate gamble for happiness.

But I didn't lose my skills through disuse. I am still the ventriloquist. And now, if your gag is still on tight, you can listen and I will throw you into Lock, Cell and Sly.

Part Three

BRIDE

1 Ghost Doll

—Barbarella! Barbarella? Come here and have a look at this. You will be surprised. Look. Do you see—I had flesh but now I'm plastic, just like you. Is that you there, standing by my shoulder? All in white, you're the bride, the beautiful bride, radiant with the light, all glowing pure as lilies

—Dim, what are you on about? Come away from the mirror.

—No, Barbarella. I have to stay here, making my own acquaintance

—Stop calling me Barbarella.

—But that's what I've always called you

—No. I'm Lock. Come here and lie down.

The bed came up to stare at me, the sheets as pure as Barbarella's white gown. Then it swallowed me. The sheets wrap around, they swathe and swaddle and smother because the white is not for me, it doesn't want me it wants Barbarella because she is the one who is spotless and her perfection is complete and real and primary. She had it first.

I tried to tell her, but she was rolling me up in them like a bandage. Tears started to crystallise on the face which I was wearing. The face looked then as if it had been left out in the rain—I could tell this because Barbarella was wearing glasses and I could see the reflection as she bent over me. The little face, like the fallen blossom on the lawn, speckled with rain and little pepper grains of dirt, no doubt. Is the rot coming for me?

Barbarella liked the tears. She'd always been one for cruelty. I had never had a friend who was otherwise. She liked the tears so much she was kissing me. Not kissing me better; kissing me worse. For better or worse Barbarella the bride was kissing me.

—You may kiss the bride, I said.

—Dimity, she answered, her fingers tracing a scar running straight down my navel and into my knickers, do you see this scar? It's not long for this world, Dimity. Because I am going to wipe it off you. I am going to make you a perfect body. And when I've made it for you I will make sure that you have it forever. And then, only then, will you be my bride. When you are perfect.

—No, Barbarella, I can never be perfect. You're wrong about that. And why are you wearing this gold ring?

—Because I'm Lock, not Barbarella.

—Lock?

—Yes. Your rescuer. Your white knight in shining armour. That type of scenario. I'm going to put the pieces back together again.

—Pieces.

There were pieces which fit. She was lying over me, wriggling to get them together. Her white dress was spread all about. She was nestling with me in the flower.

The gauze everywhere, and the mist in the air. And then I realised what was happening.

—You're a ghost!

—No, Dimity.

More kisses. The ghost was quivering over me in the warm air. Her breath flew off on it like so many cabbage moths, eddying unpredictably, unevenly on the currents. Simmering white, the phantom was about to evanesce. Heat waves shuddering off her back, Barbarella my ghost doll rose off to heaven in a long moan. But I recalled, she deserved it because she'd been through hell. She had played sati in a horrific blaze of lost loves and now she was back to haunt me.

2 Lock

I couldn't believe it when I opened the door and saw her. I mean, she was never a pretty kid before, but she looked okay. Funny body—all angles. Good for modelling but not much else—no meat on her. She had nice big dark eyes. Olive skin. Long slender legs and next to no bum. She had her assets.

But now—hell, I never saw a woman with scarring that bad. I even thought I'd have to refer her to someone else. Someone whose reputation had been built on challenges like hers. Someone who had experience in totally rebuilding a body, putting it back together almost from scratch.

I'd reversed a few holocausts in my time but never anything as extreme as this. Most of my work had been touch-ups—little improvements. I hardly ever totally overhauled a body from top to toe. I wondered if I could handle it.

But then I remembered the way I'd felt about her when I first found her again, up on stage in that weird freak show. Possessive. I'd wanted to get hold of her. Watching her with her hand stuck up the back of that bizarre doll she was manipulating, I was bowled over by this incredible feeling of wanting to control her like that, wanting to sit her down on my knee and make her do whatever I fancied. God knows why she brought that out in me. She wasn't the only one to bring it out. There were plenty of girls out there that touched it. You know the type. The sort that ache with their own vulnerability. They've got this waif's delicacy. Little thunderclouds, scared of their own black nerve-crackling centres. That sort always made the hair on the back of my hands sit right up. I'd have to pursue them. They weren't that hard to get, usually. But they were bloody hard to keep. Always getting lost, or losing it on drugs, deserting or suiciding, or submitting to others who wanted them too. Controlling them was easy, but they always ended up vanquished by their own weaknesses.

I'd give them everything. Put them up in fully-furnished apartments, pay all the bills. Feed them. Pet them. Dress them up. Take them out. Introduce them to people who could help them. And of course I'd make them better. For free, I'd enhance what they had. Straighten any little kinks in the fawnish beauty which they were born with. Smooth their noses, round out their upper lips with collagen, highlight their chins or cheekbones, pin their ears back, eradicate any little lumps, scars, freckles, wrinkles, birthmarks or blemishes, plump out their little breasts. When they left me, or when I moved them out, they left perfect. Better than God created them.

As I said, Dim really brought the feeling out in me. That's why I'd gone up to her after the show. She had the makings of something really extraordinary. I knew that if she gave me free rein she could really become someone special. She was just tall enough, and definitely lean enough, to model. The glossies liked girls like her. Once I'd cleaned up the angles in her face and brought them into proportion, with enough hair and makeup work they could photograph her wearing anything. She had potential.

More than that though. I remembered her. The child she'd been at school. The complaisant little bitch. She was the grubby kid with the scruffy brown plait and freckles who sat still when I burned her arm with a cigarette lighter. The same kid who didn't cry out when I buried her up to her neck in sand. The kid who didn't dob me in when I tied her up against a tree and water-bombed her relentlessly for fifteen minutes. The kid who uncomplainingly ate the stew of worms and chokos that I forced on her. I didn't even get busted for playing doctors and nurses with her, and I'd taken that pretty far. She'd been my captive, and I'd utterly controlled her. All that when we were both too young for it to be real any more.

And then there she was again, up on the stage in that tawdry sideshow, temptation supreme, because I knew she'd submit to anything. You could still see it in her eyes. Years since I'd last seen her, but you could still pick it. That crushed look, the beaten-before-you-begin bruising in her expression. She'd made it part of her act, and it gave her this twisted kind of star quality. I saw her up there and I just wanted to get her home and start work on her, put my stamp on her. Give her to herself, the best she could possibly be.

When I gave her my card I realised she was too scared of me to ever call me. She knew I'd have power over her. She was reluctant to give herself up to it, but part of her wanted to, I could tell.

So when I saw her in my surgery it was like a windfall. The apple that had tempted you, which you'd tried to pick but couldn't bend the branch low enough to pluck, or bounce it enough to knock it down. Then all of a sudden you're hanging about under the tree and you find it there, waiting for you, but in the meantime it's got a big black chunk out of it where it's hit the ground and lain there long enough to ferment. After the initial shock, I realised that I still wanted her. I decided I might never have a challenge as worthy as this again. I was going to get this apple and reconstitute her, make her so perfect she'd look artificial.

She had the same eyes. The same Bambi brown eyes. Except they were denuded of lashes. I don't think I ever saw anything as sad as that in my whole life, the poor eyes blinking and staring and welling with tears, obscenely unedged.

So I took her home.

And over time, I made her my masterpiece. She was my crowning achievement as a plastic surgeon. I got a lot of mileage out of her at conferences and in journals, and I don't exaggerate when I say that she got me where I am today. I gave her a great start too, totally re-creating her from the mess she confronted me with that day at surgery. But like that type of girl always does, she totally stuffed it up. She could have been anyone or anything if she'd only let me finish the job for her. But she had to live out her shitty little destiny, despite my best attempts. It was as if she wasn't capable of imagining a future that wasn't hashed up.

She wouldn't go out. Even once I had her face finished she wouldn't go out. I'd done a lovely job on it. I'd sit and look at her for hours when she was asleep, marvelling at it. I didn't make her classically beautiful—I'd made sure to steer clear of the ice princess look which the yuppie girls and the rich socialites were always striving for. It always looked fake. Plus it dated. Nor was she a voluptuous thick-lipped brunette. She was more of a perfectly proportioned girl next door, albeit with a difference. A child woman, with bone structure to die for. She could have walked down a street and turned only one head, but that head would have been the head of a connoisseur—someone who knew beauty back to front, and could pick it anywhere. She wasn't a cliché, in other words. She was exquisite, original, compelling, and queer. The beauty I made for her was the sort that came out on the second or third look, and it got better the longer you looked.

But she still wouldn't go out. In a longsleeved shirt and pants the other scars wouldn't have showed. Her face, neck and hands were fully reconstructed, and her hair had grown back. But she was terrified to go out.

She lay around in the apartment, day in, day out. She cried a lot. And she was crazy. She kept calling me names, talking utter nonsense. When I tried to find out what had happened to her she'd rattle on for ages, if she'd speak at all, about her mother being a sati. Complete crap.

But she was as complaisant as ever. She'd come to bed when she was asked. I'd never fucked anyone so unresponsive. It was as if she was so detached from the experience that she didn't even feel it. She never once tried to seduce me. It wouldn't have been hard—she had the quality which touched that nerve in me, so that I only had to look at her once to be overpoweringly ardent. If I'd been her I'd have played with it. I'd have teased, withheld, domineered. I would have savoured the control. She never did that. She obviously wasn't interested in manipulating me. Sometimes I wonder now what she thought of me. What she felt about me. I never asked her, since it didn't seem important. I was mad about her, and I knew she'd do anything I wanted. That was the sum of the relationship.

Until she opposed me. I couldn't believe it was happening. I couldn't believe that this child woman, with the huge submissive sad eyes, would say no to me. It happened on the full moon. I had her in bed. She lay across the sheets, slender and taut as a cord tossed there. Most of the work was finished. I was smoothing her skin with my hands, admiring the new flawlessness. I was congratulating myself—where the moon stroked her she was immaculate, and the light glanced off her as if from a polished surface. There was no scarring to mar the effect.

—You look like a doll lying there. A metal doll.

—The doll is sleeping—see her eyes are shut?

—A Barbie doll? That's who you see isn't it? That's who you talk to.

—No, not Barbie. Her name is Barbarella.

I rolled over, suspended my face over hers. Her liquid eyes were molten silver now, shudderingly they blinked in their net of new lashes. The pillow glowed white, with the strands of her hair, longer now, fanning out dark as spilt treacle across it. She let me kiss her.

—You look like Barbie now.

She gazed up, impassive.

—Just about everything's done. I'm nearly finished.

I put my palm over her breast. Except these. They're next. Not for the scarring. We did that already, remember? All clean now. But you can't be Barbie in an A cup, can you?

I kissed her there. She lay still. With my head on her ribcage I smiled at her nipples, glistening with spit. Then I shifted to the end of the bed and brought her foot up to my lips.

—And one other thing before we're done . . .

I traced the shape of the ugly tattoo she'd had done on her heel. Tacky shit—no doubt the relic of her circus days.

—We're taking this off.

A sudden current of life surged through her. It was like the silver moonlight had converted to lightning, cracked her head and coursed straight down her spine and through her heel, which rebounded so forcefully in my hand that she kicked my mouth. The cool air became charged. She had raised her head from the pillow to look at me. I smiled, stroking her foot with one hand and holding it firm with the other.

—It can't stay. It spoils the effect. Once I've finished I don't want any leftover muck. I've put a lot of work in on you and I'm not having it debased. Don't worry—I can take this tattoo off so you'll never know it was there.

A shudder went through her, and she said, No.

—No? What do you mean, no?

—No. I'm keeping it.

—Why?

—You can have everything else. But I'm keeping that.

—No you're not. It's coming off tomorrow.

She kicked me. I was amazed at the power in it. After all, she had been lying around for months and months, often in recovery from surgery, and she hadn't had a lot of exercise. But she kicked like a wild beast. Her foot contacted my mouth and bashed a big hole in my lip where she'd jagged it on my teeth. In a spurt of blood and pain I pulled her towards me. She was flailing with her feet and arms, scratching. When I put my hand up near her face she twisted in a lashing of hair and bit it so hard it drew more blood. She had blood on her lips. She looked like a demon, writhing and grimacing and clawing wherever she could. My doe had turned devil. I couldn't believe the transformation.

Shit I was angry. The astonishment was so quickly converted to adrenalin that I'd warped her arms back behind her and pinned her to the bed before I knew what I was doing.

Holding her down, I told her, You're lucky I didn't smack you stupid, Dim. But we don't want to spoil the work now, do we? I don't believe you want to go back to square one. Do you, Dim?

She was still again. Stretched out under me in star formation, waiting. I did something I'd never done before. I tied her to the bed. I left her tied there for three days. She never once complained, never cried. She just lay there, like a martyr on the cross. For three days she made no sound. On the fourth day she started talking. She was delirious. Madder than she'd ever been before. I started to worry that I'd actually derailed her mind—but really she was pretty fucked in the head before she even walked into my surgery. When it was clear that she was sick, I untied her. She had red rings around her wrists and ankles, like stigmata.

I showered her, towelled her dry, and got her clothes on. It was like dressing a dummy—she was utterly stiff and resistant. Uncaring. I worked her into a bra, a pair of knickers, a longsleeved cream smock. I checked that the marks on her wrists and ankles had faded. I put some shoes on her feet. Then I sat her down in a chair and cooked her dinner. I had to spoon-feed it to her. She would only eat a little bit.

Fuck knows what made me do that to her. I've been cruel in the past but this was something extra. Must have been about the way I felt about her. I *felt* something extra. So everything was enhanced, blown up and out of proportion, expanded. My desire, my occasional cruelties, my drive for her perfection, my professionalism. Everything about me.

After the meal she slowed down a bit. She started to make more sense. Not that much more though. Something had turned in that head of hers. She was gorgeous but mad as all hell. Not normal. Not surprising really, considering her upbringing and that bizarre patch with the circus. She hadn't exactly had a normal life, that was for sure.

She gave me cause to regret a whole lot of things. I wished I'd taken that tattoo off her when she was tied down and I had the chance. A big regret was that for the first time in my entire life I was in love—with her. Desperately. And I was beginning to think that she hated me. Or herself. Or both. Because she started to abuse herself. I don't know where she was getting the valium but she was getting it, among other things. She drank all the alcohol I had in the house before I realised and stopped restocking it. The worse thing though was when she stopped eating altogether, only a day after I untied her. She started to starve herself. She starved herself to the point of death. There was even a moment where I thought she *had* died. There's me, driving myself crazy trying to force-feed this lunatic girl, bawling my eyes out because I'm terrified this girl's going to die and that without her I'll die too. I regret that loss of control more than anything. That woman made a baby out of me. I don't quite forgive it.

3 Sunken Treasure

It is dark in here with all the blinds down and we are living inside my skull with the lids shut. Me and Barbarella and sometimes the Warlock, who comes to hold us to our promises. Did I promise that I would try to be perfect? Barbarella tells me yes, yes I did make that earnest promise and she sneers when I cry and tell her I can't do it now.

Barbarella tells me to hold my breath and then my body, absent of air, will look its best. We don't eat. Perfection does not require fuel. It is pure and nothing need be added.

We haven't been in the sun for a long time. Our legs are long and thin and waxy as plastic. When we cross them they whisper their chafe. There are corrugations along our torsos—when we have to navigate the huge oceans these ribbings will hold our barge stable.

When the Warlock finds us at the end of the day we are lying side by side on our barge. Our buttocks are bruised from the lying there. We have been wrapped in our sheets like mummies in their bandages, and calm as if dead we repose all the livelong day. These four spikes lined up in a row are our pelvises. We pretend that they are the portcullis and the Warlock will never be able to pass them without impaling himself.

The Warlock is often angry when he comes up to our tower and finds us together. I am scared that he will throw Barbarella out the window. Or me. Except he cherishes me too much to throw me away to the thorn-bush. He doesn't want to feel the power which he does, so sometimes he hurts me so that we know who is boss. I am just the jewel in his crown. Coveted coverlet courtesan me.

When I am eating the pearls he is angry. He knows they are eaten, even though he has not found the hiding place. He knows because the whole world swims into the deep blue sea and won't come out. The barge is sunk right to the bottom. He is coaxing to the coral reef which won't let him into the sea. There is the endless floating wonder there where I can drift as quiet as can be, waiting to meet my old friend down there. Surely that old friend still remembers me.

I call out to my friend and my voice is only a tiny vibration bubbling through the vast. The Warlock is back. The Warlock interrupts. The Warlock knows he is the captain of this here ship and no skindiving pirates need apply (he means my friend). He hangs over the barge.

—Dim?

—Yes. It is.

—Dimity, how many did you have? Listen to me. Dim, how many?

There is a swooshing roll of ocean and my head

lolls with it, abandoned as the seaweed. The smoothest pleasure makes me laugh slow and low and my neck overarches so that the laugh goes swirling up to the glassy perpetual-motion surface and pops into air before the Warlock's face.

—What is it, Warlock?

—My name is Lock, not Warlock.

He spits this out. Useless: there is enough water already. More laughing is surfacing so he reaches down to the barge and shakes his sunken courtesan by her bandaged shoulders and tells her, To get like this you must have taken a whole packet! And then he prises open the clam to look inside. But all the pearls have been swallowed and he has to go up for air, empty-handed.

It isn't long before he is back with a new cargo. There is a spoonful of salt that is forced into my clam until all the delicate sides are pursed and stinging and retracting. He has the whole head up by the chin and the neck can't help but gulp and set off the tumult so that everything is torrid or torrents and there is the inside coming back out and they are dredged up. I mean the pearls. Except they are unrecognisable now.

He lets me go and I recline once more next to Barbarella. There is food which he wants me to eat but I pretend to be asleep. He is not ashamed to force it though. Like the salt. He isn't embarrassed to ram it down. But I have my own salt. With two fingers when his back is turned I make my own reversals. How can he tell the difference between one sick and the next?

When he lies with me the portcullis slows him. It

bruises if he tries to slide. But he is not ashamed to force it, as before.

There is no time any more. Barbarella and I have been cast off into the hugeness of the universe and there is only continuity. I do notice though that my friend has started to hover at a distance. I welcome, but that friend does not approach. There is only the flickering at the murky end of my capacity to see through the boundlessness of ocean, the little fishflock movements that let me know who is near. I invite.

—Please come.

The Warlock thinks I am speaking to him. He is vulnerable because I have requested. He puts hands.

—I want to go now.

Warlock blocks my attempt to communicate with death by planting his muscled suction-cup lips on my face, and clinging there as the tides surge impossibly close. At last though, my friend approaches close enough for me to look into the face of the end. The face looks like Morgan's where it hovers in wavering fins and spiralled trails of air going up to surface, backing against the currents over the Warlock's shoulder. For a long time it wafts there, in its element, engaging me.

—Please take me.

But death refuses me. A big NO of oxygen mushrooms in the subaqueous light and death watches me take it in, before changing direction and ruddering swiftly sideways in retreat. Death vanishes in the white water at the edge of my ragged mind, leaving me to the misapprehension under which the Warlock is labouring as he lays me flat to the deck.

I realise that I will have to keep living. There are still too many lives left for me to sink.

So when the Warlock lies beached at my side I tell him I am hungry.

The delight splits his face as the crystal ball had split the head of Antonio Houdini Grieg. It is the beginning of the end for him. It is not long before he loses this part of the game.

4 Lock Sees the Thorns

When she started to eat and get her strength back I treated it as a miracle. I decided she must be in love with me. Because for the first time since she'd presented herself to my surgery, she'd asked me for something. First to make love to her, then to feed her. Every other thing I'd done for her I'd done because it was necessary, or because she seemed to need or want it, or often enough because I needed or wanted it. But now for the first time I was responding to her requests. I felt totally high for a week.

It took a while for her to come back. The whole time she was as sweet as pie. Gradually she got stronger. She was still skinny but she didn't look like she had a terminal disease any more. She didn't ask for things again, but something had changed. It was like some spirit, some part of her that had receded after whatever disaster flung her into my life, had come back in.

I may have been kidding myself when I thought that it was love. But I didn't take any chances. I still deadlocked her inside every day, just in case she thought she might do a runner. Because I never quite trusted her. It was hard to treat her as other than my captive, since she'd played that role so long.

But nothing could have prepared me for what she did do. It was a complete spectacle. She could have done it when I was out, but she saved it up and made sure that I saw it.

It was an afternoon after work and I was making a meal in the kitchen. She came out, all dressed up like a priestess in a long cream dress. She'd taken the flowers from the vase in the bedroom and dressed her hair with them, and she'd put makeup on. At that moment, she was easily the most beautiful woman I had ever seen. I told her so. She laughed and came over to my side of the kitchen bench and, to my pleasure and surprise, kissed me. Then she wriggled away and stood in the centre of the living room. I stared at her standing there, islanded in her perfection. The afternoon sunlight mellowed as it hit her, swam languidly golden about her brow like a crown.

—I think you're well now. Do you?

—Well?

—You've got your health back.

—But my body is gone forever.

I laughed.

—Lucky little Dim. Lots of girls would give their left arm to have a new body like you have. And you got it for free.

She was pleating the fabric of the dress, murmuring, Surely not free, surely a price . . .

—You look like a bride standing there like that.

She looked up, sudden, numinous, new. She laughed in my face.

—Dim, I think you're well enough for us to pick up where we left off.

—Did we leave something off?

—Yes. Remember—the implants. That was the only thing left to put on. Oh, and one other thing. The tattoo has to come off.

—It does?

—Of course. You understand why, don't you?

—Yes. It isn't your signature, so it must come off your work.

—In a manner of speaking, yes.

—My charmed life is over.

—It's about to begin. When I've finished those two things I'm going to make you my wife.

—Make me?

—Not make you, silly. I can't make you do anything.

—You haven't made me already? It's not finished yet?

—I just told you. Only those two things and you're finished, except for maintenance work as time takes its toll.

—Make me. You've made me. You will make me your wife.

She let off a laugh like church music.

—I won't make you. I'll ask you. I'll ask you now. Dimity, will you be my wife?

She laughed again. Holding her left foot, she pulled her left leg up backwards to her buttocks and looked over her shoulder at the dark thread of the tattoo, winding around her heel. I was so sure she'd agree to me taking it off I didn't even care in that moment that it soiled the vision she was parading before me. I was confident that she'd want the ugly insignia removed now that she was well and in love with me—she'd do whatever I asked. I didn't even hold my breath waiting for her answer to my proposal, because I was sure she'd say yes. She would be my bride. I picked up the knife.

—Lock, she said, you keep me imprisoned in this apartment block like Rapunzel in her tower.

I laughed, and started chopping lettuce for the salad. She was evading the question. But she would still be my bride.

—And do you know what I think? she continued. I think it is time that Rapunzel left the wicked witch to her own devices and went off to find her handsome prince.

It hurt a little bit. I'd always thought that I was her handsome prince. But I thought she was joking. I got into the spirit of things.

—You want to let your hair down? Go out on the town? Come out of your ivory tower and see the real world? I'll take you out after dinner if you like. It will be the first time you've been out in more than a year.

She smiled sweetly.

—Lock, have you seen the thorns below?

—Thorns?

—Mmm.

—What thorns? There's only concrete. We're a floor above ground.

—Yes. But they will be there. The thorns. Watch.

The smile was mad. The madness of one who knew she could do what she was about to do and get away with it. God knows how she knew it. Because she paused in the centre of the room, radiant with the information, just long enough to knot my gut in a rope of yearning so powerful I dropped the knife I was holding. Then she jumped straight through the closed window. For an instant she was superimposed there as if on a mosaic, her edges luminous against the surface crazed with her impact. The surface broke the instant and flew in all directions and she was through and falling out of view. There was a huge strange delayed crash of broken glass. When I rushed to the window and looked down there was no one. Only shards of glass sprayed all around.

—Thorns, I said, clutching at the window edge until I noticed the blood laced around my thumb and index finger.

Part Four

WHALE

1 WAIF

Later on, Cell wanted to know the story. She pestered me for details. You there, sequestered in your bonds and silent, can't ask as she did. You can't even ask me, who or what is this Cell? It's not for you to query my strange uncompromising tale, its characters or its organisation. But nevertheless it is your lot to know the tale closely, intimately. You embrace the tale as those very cords buckle and circle you. Its fibres strangle and suffocate you, wad your mouth and clot your eyes. Perhaps you feel the victim of this tale just now. I recommend you, continue to keep your counsel. That way you'll learn all the missing pieces. All the little stitches in a story which I had to keep from the person unlucky enough to be cast as my sister. Of course you understand why I had to keep them from her. How could I tell anyone this tale? Who could believe it? You yourself listen no doubt because I have imposed a condition upon you, so that you cannot protest and query. This allows me to finish. In the end the gift is yours: understanding. If I let you interrupt me all the time you would never get all the pieces, you'd judge too soon, and you'd not see the reasons for it all. So let me tell you now what happened when I jumped from the tower. You alone are my confidante. Keep counsel, keep counsel.

I was a crazy creature, that's true. But I knew enough of my own destiny to take a calculated risk with the patterning of my deaths. There was no Morgan talking to me, no pressure from Barbarella. I wasn't afraid of the thorns—I knew that I could jump from the tower and live. I had already survived my two falls and there were no more left in my itinerary of deaths. Remember that I had already died six times, having also encountered death by snakebite, by drowning, starvation and fire. I intuited that I could fall that short distance to concrete without damage. Because my next death was other. So I gambled and fell and stood up and walked away. I won that bet.

I breasted the glass the way a runner breasts the ribbon across the finishing line. Launched yet again in air, I spread my arms and drew in my feet, a bedlam dove escaped from the shattered dovecote, my off-white war gown ribboned and striped with blood. I landed, joints shuddering and cracking, crouched in a nest of glass. I looked for a moment at the twirl of tattoo on my heel, unscathed though bloodied by the hacked soles of my feet, struggled up to a staggering standing pose, paused only for an instant with wild gaze, just comprehending that I had cut my arms and legs and that a gash across my breasts had spurted over my face and hair. My crown of lilies dressed my brow, redflecked. If I had seen them perhaps they would have stilled my flight. Those white flowers, speckled ruby, on the turn. But I didn't pause to consider how I looked, how mad a spectacle, how aghast a specimen, how forlorn and horrifying an escapee. I just ran for it as if this was the last life I'd ever have and the only way to get anywhere with it was to exercise those crippled feet. Bloodied footprints must have led away from the scene. Perhaps that was how he tracked me, that evil powerful Warlock who knew my fate and made it his.

I ran and ran and ran. I didn't know where I was. The huge city was strange to me, not my territory. When I had first arrived there I hadn't tarried: my mission had been to find the Warlock and implore him to mend and sustain the hideous broken body, whorled in scars and nauseating to see, which had become me. He took me up to the tower and I learned no more about the lay of the land down there in the labyrinth which was his domain. So I knew that speed and cunning were my only hope against his reconnaissance, his detailed knowledge of the maze, and his legion of familiars. When the darkness came I was a long way away from the tower. I crouched in the muggy heat of the street, huddled against the back entrance to one of the big office blocks. The driveway extended down from the ledge which harboured my crimped up body, a fluorescent-lit shaft leading to the bowels of the earth. I hung my head to cry, cupping my swollen scabrous feet in my shaking hands. Along with the wind and the air-conditioning units, I moaned and hummed and keened in the humid tunnel of the alley. Black shadows coveted my crying, streetlighting bombarded it with a peach luminescence, light breezes swollen with heat worried and badgered it.

In my grief and despair, I did a kind of stocktake.

There had not been many opportunities in my frantic existence to mourn the remarkable trajectory of my losses. They numbered many dead. Morgan and Con were dead. So were SadoMan, Tats, Antonio Houdini Grieg, Camera Lucida, Vera Amorphous and Madame Futura. The dolls and my tree snake were gone. The rainforest itself and our tenuous little house had gone up in smoke. Realising that I had no origin, I lifted my snotsmeared face to grunt my guttural lamentation at the curious night.

When I had finished crying, I began looking for some clue about the nature of the life I was trying so desperately to live. Sitting there, listening to the jazz of wind and traffic noise reverberating through the alley, marvelling at the wet and smelly air on my lacerated skin after months of air-conditioning, I realised that the spiral serpent slumbered. Maybe I was just too scared to summon it any more. I looked up at the droning grids of air-conditioning units, dustclogged and filthy, and said, The thing is, Barbarella, everyone I've ever known is dead. The only person who managed to survive in tandem with this curse was the Warlock, and only because he's as bad as the curse itself. Why didn't I see that he was Morgan's right hand?

There was no answer.

—Barbarella?

The breezes twirled past me with a scurry of litter on their trail. Still Barbarella, like you, kept close her counsel.

—Barbarella, I continued, provoking her. Don't you

see? If I am some fake thing that Morgan brewed up, he's here to finish the job. The job of making me. The fakest thing I can possibly be. Plastic, just like you.

I waited. It was amazing that Barbarella's competitive spirit did not fire up like a blowtorch at that statement, balding me anew. She was as dumb as my four year old self. For the rest of the night I sat in that alley, crusted in my own blood, and talked to a ghost doll that had gone silent. Did I, in wanton disregard, slice out her viperous tongue with a shard of glass when I launched my new identity as streetkid? I'd never know what muted my Barbarella.

At dawn the next morning I remained, spent and hoarse, in the same foetal curl. I had called, cajoled, begged and even attempted to blackmail and threaten Barbarella, and now my voice was slack with the trying. I felt that I would never speak again because I was at last more thoroughly and completely abandoned than ever before. Even the sight of my tattoo wavered before my eyes in a scurf of blood and dirt, offering nothing. It was just at the point where the sickly city sun proffered its first rays that a woman wearing dirty overalls came out of the back of one of the buildings opposite, hefting a load of rubbish bound up in bulging black plastic bags. She heaved the bags into the waste station next to the service driveway and turned to see me crouched in the doorway opposite. What did she see but a freak, a blood-bespattered and tearstained refugee in a sullied sacrificial robe?

In a snarl of fear she drew back, dropping the lid

of the waste station in a clang that rocked the alley.

I saw her as a predator. Of course I was no more than prey in those days. More terrified than she, I leapt up and raced desperately to the end of the alley.

This made the point forcefully. I mean that it gave me my bearing in this new environment. I realised that to distract me from the silencing of my ghost doll, there was the business of survival. Once again I laid my mourning aside and got on with the business of sustaining myself in this, my seventh life. There followed a period of scavenging, hiding and terror.

Yes, terror. Because even if most of my past had gone up in flames, the Warlock was alive. Despite the courage that hurled me through the glass side of the tower and out into the thorny beginning of another world, I could not vanquish this terror. Understand that for months I had spoken to no one other than the Warlock. He had become the only other known individual on earth. The world I knew had been razed to the ground, and he ruled the desert which was left. The apartment was his control tower, rising up out of that barrenness. Wherever I went now in the maze of the city, I feared that his sophisticated surveillance would isolate me. I knew that in the end he would hunt me down. That was one reason why I hid in the central business district. The buildings were so high and dense here, I reasoned that he couldn't get a birdseye view of me.

I couldn't afford for the Warlock to find me, because against him I would be worse than defenceless. His powers were great and I was very afraid that he would quickly pinpoint my location and drag me back to the tower. I suspected him of traffic with the ghost of my mother. Between them, they would restrain me. It was unlikely that I would escape if they ever tied me up again. So I constantly changed my position, my style of movement, my very ways. Like a person camping next to a waterhole harbouring a giant crocodile, I studiously developed no routine, and made tiny dashing forays to the bank of the danger zone only when I had to.

Despite my precautions, I had reason to believe that the Warlock was tracking me. I heard his voice in the wuthering of ill-omened winds between the office blocks, hollowly calling my name. In the purple sky at dusk, the shadows of flying foxes glimpsed in the rectangular gaps between the soaring buildings were evidence of his demonic surveillance. From beneath sheets of old newspaper, I heard their squeaks and pips, knowing that they were relaying information back to the control tower. Whenever I noticed them, I fled the looming shadows which suggested the Warlock's presence on my trail.

So I led the life of an alien, never showing my face by day, never venturing to public places where the Warlock might locate me. I avoided contact with all the new individuals who now became apparent as I navigated the wider world. Those who glimpsed me stared at my filthy cream dress in surprise until I ran away. Each week, I grew dirtier. My feet and elbows scaled, my hair knotted, my lips cracked and a hundred minor ailments pained me as my immune system struggled with my new lifestyle. My cuts took a long time to heal, and several got infected. When the stubborn wounds finally closed, I was left with a body which bore the marks of the fall, webbed in fine scars which reminded me painfully of SadoMan. The body which I now had was one step on from the Warlock's creation, second-hand, somehow used. There was some comfort in this. This body, as always, was filled with subliminal voices. Voices which I could not project just now, but which I could feel butting inside the hollow vessel which was myself. I held this disputatious cacophony of voices inside me like other bodies hold cancers, keeping them secret from myself.

There was something else that was new. And its positivity was a paradox. When I jumped out of that window I took my life back from the Warlock. In a strange way it was an act of control. So now, even if I was mad, I was saner than I had been for many months. I was running my own life, even if it was a life on the run. I still had the promise of power, my tattoo.

Perhaps this was why I was able to approach the next part of my destiny with a greater measure of coherence than I had exhibited in the last. Even though I lived as a vagabond for many months, I was less scattered. If Morgan looked on she must have known that I was now primed for something. She probably snickered in her prescient exile, knowing that this new waif me was one who could mount a large-scale seduction over a long period of time, one who could stage a determined play for survival, one who could take risks and balance a fine line of deceit for very high stakes. This person was ready for the curse to really kick in. I had been fully prepared. Now the seeds of my dire childhood, dormant so long that I had forgotten them, finally sent out their probes. I was about to meet the people who would allow that stock of infertility, faithlessness and madness to surface.

I discovered the sanctuary of the office blocks quite by chance. It was summer when I jumped, and I was lucky not to need shelter from the bitter winter nights of that city. The weather was on my side. However, once I had picked my meals from the garbage bins at the back of the office blocks, I would spend all of each night in an anxious and paranoid sweat, watching for shadows and sounds and signs of the Warlock's many familiars. One day, hardly considering the consequences, I followed my instinct and slipped into one of the towers. Inside, I realised that it was possible to avoid both cleaners and security guards with very little ingenuity. I could spend the nights locked up safe in the huge concrete blocks, muzzled in carpet and sealed in reflective glass, quietly waiting and watching, stilling my breathing until I scarcely could be diagnosed as a living being. In these giant sepulchres I was sure I could escape the notice of my progenitrix and her servant. Just to make extra certain, I played dead. Who would want to hound a corpse?

I did not know what would end this period. I could not imagine it ending, but it was clearly untenable. It took another person to end it for me. The person I told you of just before. Yes, it was Cell, coming nightly to the office block, where I was sleeping. She had flow. Yet her whole body was integral, radiant and utterly cohesive in its individuality.

Where Antonio Houdini Grieg had exhibited pure ego, Cell showed me another identity. It was magnificently simple, irreducibly pure, self-contained yet all-embracing. It looked so beautiful to me, fissured as I was with voices and ghosts.

I wanted her identity so much it brought stinging tears to my eyes. I stalked her for it. There were so many hours which I spent suspended at the edge of her consciousness, holding my breath, observing her and trying to fathom a connection. I clung to every breath and shiver and bead of sweat which her body released. I studied these and every other aspect of her which I could read.

She was my fascination. I suppose she was my reason for living. There wasn't really any other because my life had become that of a cheap forager, the frightened quarry of more powerful beasts.

Eventually, after watching her for some weeks, I narrowed in on her. I opened the door which separated us and propelled myself into her life. If she saw me coming, she must have seen me like this.

What is that?

Who was that?

Clinging to the pale pinky beige of the wall, painted only that month, shimmering in the toxic odours emanating steady, invisible, from the new paint. Grey grained and streaked with blue, splayed cannily against the carpet, wrapped in that insurgent smell of carpet glue and acrylic. Wafting ectoplasmic from the grate overhead, a spy sliding stealthy as bacteria on the draught, invisible the moment you looked.

Surely just another tic of the complex, just another sensation like the asthma, like the queasy stomach, the running nose, the dry mouth. A quirk of the vision. Sick building syndrome—just one more symptom.

Cell knew that the building had its eccentricities. She'd often see, out of the corner of her eye, rays of sunlight trapped inside during the late evenings of daylight saving. They'd joust desperately with the glass. Every evening, the bedraggled air, weary from its daylong conditioning, threaded its deadened eddies in corners of rooms. The fluorescent lights clicked and flickered uncertainly, slyly. Sometimes they would buzz like trapped and despairing flies. But there were no flies in here. They weren't allowed in. Where I trailed my fingertips along the spotless laminated surfaces in the rooms, they dehydrated from the chemical detergents which the cleaners used. Looking at them, I was reminded of the concentric circles in the cross-sectional trunks of felled trees. Cell told Sly how she tasted the residue of ennui on the mouthpiece of the telephone when she held it close to her lips.

But this other aspect of the building was less predictably contemporary corporate architecture at its worst. This one was special, archaic, touching in its evocation of a lost past when spirits whirled real in homes, made the air turgid in workplaces, wreaked havoc or shed bounty, offered both terror and guardianship. This aspect was like a haunting.

There lived, in the corners of Cell's big wet eyes, a phantasm. And the phantasm, whenever she pursued it with her full gaze, vanished. Remember that I didn't like the open space. Not the broad panorama for me. I dwelt only in the nexus, in the angles, in the joins. As if I needed a frame. Because the undifferentiated field of full vision was anathema to me. Cell, puzzling her phantom's elusiveness, wondered if perhaps its delicacy wouldn't bear close scrutiny, wouldn't withstand the bald savannah of plain gazing. She was right. I needed protection. It had become my habit to seek cover, camouflage, corners. I was a master of deceit. Cell noted that the phantasm, like a chameleon, traded its identity for that of its surrounds. It preferred safety to those other commodities—individuality, singularity, recognition, admiration even—that others sought and even fought for.

From what Cell could glean, this unlooked for aspect of the building was human, frail, evasive. Like a gecko, pallid and transparent with huge overawed and watchful eyes, this aspect clung to surfaces, and moved sometimes with ponderous secrecy, other times with the flash we call speed. Mostly, it was invisible. But did it, like a gecko, advance cunningly towards some goal, some ultimate gratification? Did it look to satisfy some tiny, natural but frightening appetite? Perhaps its delicacy, its fragility and apparent fear, were the veil of a disproportionate and implacable greed.

Perhaps. Cell remembered Sly's insistence that those who were quiet and evasive were something more, were planning something, observing, withholding themselves for a reason. If it's true that the meek shall inherit the earth, we have to watch out for those shrinking ones who never seem to want anything. Because it's all a front. That's what he would say, glaring at the chrysalid coil of a man sleeping in the doorway of a vacant house.

So if Cell knew she was being haunted, she didn't know what haunted her. She wouldn't find out until the night the door opened, and everything changed. It was one of those points in any life where the switch flicks back and the old world is unhinged. Just like that. One door inching open, the Butterfly Effect. Tiny wings flicking at a point in time. One small event leading on to large-scale turbulence.

But I said I'd show you Cell. I meant that I would give her to you in the best and fullest way—the way that only I in my precocious skill could manage. I meant that I would not only describe her to you, but throw you her voice in all its subtlety and intricacy, rich in the very tones and timbres that make her unique. Remember? Or are you so trussed up in the ties I have imposed that you have forgotten my promise? Perhaps there is some evasion here. I know that I am scared to do Cell, scared to take her voice and toss it to you, my captive. I suppose that is because Cell more than my own mother is part of myself. She is the only part of myself which both loved and hated me with any clarity, and it makes her the most dangerous part that there can be. It is a hard task to untangle her voice from my own, define her dangerous contrary sister's tongue and give it separate life. There's always the risk that she will denounce me. Chary of jeopardising my precious tale, I am almost reluctant to fulfil my promise. But I want your faith, and I know faith is won not compelled. I promised to throw you Lock. And so I have. But now that you've heard Lock, I'll do as I said, and throw you Cell. Remember that I have been true to my word. Now listen. This is how Cell saw it.

2 Cell

I was sitting behind the laminated expanse of desk, the PC at my right. I was a fluorescent island in the darkened office. I felt myself spotlit, whitepink. The odd squeals and groans of the midnight wind in the elevator chute were like the chorus to the squeaks and inhalations at the other end of the phone.

My mind wasn't on it—it was taking a long time to finish him off and even though he was getting that percussive click in the back of his throat he still had a way to go so I was trying to get my mind focused on the task I had him engaged *and I just can't I just can't wait any more* and it was working: there was a whinnying sound and we were that much closer to the finishing line thank Christ but then I noticed that the door to the office was opening up as slow as a deeply drawn breath *o what are you DOING baby?* and I'm hyperventilating with the handset pressed hard against my kisser *and when I give you* head spinning, eyes on the crack. It's spreading slowly slowly *faster faster* I'm praying it won't be trouble *ooo you big bad boy you* fear: harrowing me and I gasp *o please please please* sweet angels, protect me!

Desperately plying the distance between myself and

my interlocutor with that ready flatterer, the moist end of my loose tongue finally letting him loose from the rope of dirty talk and I get him off, get him off the phone as the face comes into the crack, heartshaped and astonished, narrowed in on me at the same time as the howl at the other end funnelled down on me and I hang him up, sling him onto my hook, cut him off, sock him with my mindless purr of dial tone and ask, Who the *bloody hell* are you?

— . . . Dimity.

—What are you doing here?

—I sleep here.

—What are you, a streetkid?

She didn't answer. But she sidled cautiously into the room and shut the door. I stared. What a mess. What a delightful spooky little mess she was. Dreadlocked hair, skin smudged in dirt and pasty under the fluoros, stickthin limbs covered with scratches and bruises. A weird filthy gown that might have once been white, covered in food stains and grot and what looked like dried blood, hung off her in tatters. Staring out of the mess, the most elfin pretty little face and gigantic liquid dark eyes. And she moved with the grace of a performer, a stealthy feline step that held me in thrall. Irresistible, feral, she intrigued and charmed me. I put out one hand, partly to calm her, partly in an impulse to pet her.

3 The Ocean

Cell. She was everything that I wasn't. Rounded, fluid, dimpled. Greenyblue eyes that shone and welcomed. A woman's body—voluptuous, shapely, golden and lightly dusted with freckles. She had kindness, wit, cheek, gentility and sentimentality. She was sensuous, stable and genuine. Her borders were clear, like a diaphanous aura that surrounded her. But they were permeable. She could let people in. And she knew also how to let them out.

I thought her utterly delectable. The woman who had everything. But she didn't, it turned out.

I became close to Cell extremely quickly. I thought of her as someone I was fated to know, which must have been true. It was no ordinary fate, that's for sure.

I was curious about her. I wanted to know everything about her. She had no reservations about telling me, frankly answering any question, however intimate. In talking to her I had my first glimpse of those conversations which are supposed to be so common to women, where everything they'd ever felt or experienced got dredged up on one extended tide of mutuality. It was a somewhat twisted glimpse, and as usual, the twisting was my fault. For in this case, it was Cell's tide which carried us along, since we really only explored the wide range of *her* feelings and experiences, since I didn't want to tell her too much. Something in my battered consciousness warned me not to stretch her credulity. Thankfully, Cell was so strong and supportive that my silences were borne up and became listening rather than evasion, my evasions themselves elevated to the falterings of extreme honesty. Marvel at the transformative power of a woman who could effect this dream of connection. We approximated our friendship through her generosity, tact and willingness to believe in it long before it ever existed in any real sense. Perphaps if I had really opened out to her I would have had the gift of those truly mutual conversations, for the first time in my entire life. Cell may even have been able to heal me. But I decided that it was too dangerous, and if evasion would always live at the core of our friendship it was the price I had to pay for safety. Why didn't I see that the price would be too high?

Late at night, holed up in the offices, Cell told me about her past. She told me about her parents, her hordes of brothers, sisters, cousins, her friends and lovers. Like two teenagers, we sat by the phone and waited for it to ring. In between administering to her clients, she would share her magical tongue with me. I drank in her stories.

She was happy. She had a lover called Sly. She described him to me in terms of his hands.

—Sly. He knew. If he put a hand on me it was as if the place was made to receive it, like two pieces of a puzzle. His hands knew where to go—I told them nothing but they had been there before.

—Maybe they had. Do you believe in past lives?

Cell had to think about that one. Perhaps. I don't know. I never thought about it. Do you?

—Sometimes I do. I get the feeling sometimes that my life has been lived before. That I am repeating something . . .

The phone was ringing.

Cell had a business. She worked out of the office block, talking dirty to complete strangers. She'd done a deal with the company who used the office during the daytime, gave them a cut. They operated the phone number for their information services to clients during the day, and leased it to her for her use at night. The clients paid the charges through their phone bills. Very discreet—how they liked it. Cell had actually made enough money bringing them off to buy herself a boat. She lived at the marina. She had high plans which she loved to detail to me. One was that she was going to travel around the world. When she could talk Sly into leaving his job she was going to spend the rest of her life in the sun, dandled in the lap of the tropics in a long hug of ocean. She'd live off her investments, her squirrelled amounts in various bank accounts, her own labour and her wits. She'd never have to talk dirty again (unless she felt like it).

—You do this every night?

—Most.

—You're out all night?

—Not all night. Only until two-thirty. Things taper off after that.

—No one minds?

—What? Me being out?

—Yes.

—I suppose not.

—He doesn't mind? Your lover?

—God no. He works nights too. He's away now, anyway. What about you, do you stay here every night?

—Yes.

—No one knows?

—Only you. I have to avoid the cleaners in the evening and the security people during the night. It's not too hard.

Cell squinted at me, a beneficent narrowing. I could see her assessment—generous but honest. Me so thin. My face was pinched, quite literally. As if someone had squashed it either side of those perfect cheekbones. She took in my eyes, floating above two deep dark crescents. My olive skin pallid, from either exhaustion or malnutrition or both. Something in her just ached to protect me, nourish me. Take me home and feed me up a bit, so that I'd lose that hunted look.

But she wasn't ready to do that yet. She was still enclosed. I hadn't yet sidled up and under her skin. She took me to the ocean instead.

It took a lot to get me out of hiding during the day. But Cell was determined. After I had stood her up several times, she gave up on meeting me by day, realising that I had a phobia about being seen outside in the light. She took a lateral approach. One night she stayed up with me until dawn, closing her ears to my objections.

—No, she kept saying, you need to get out of here. All this air-conditioning and pollution and grubbing around these city streets is making you look like shit. Your skin's horrific. You need a break. Shut up and listen to me.

She blocked the door when I tried to dash past her.

Just before dawn she put her jacket over my head and bundled me out of the building, as if she knew that I had to go incognito. Once at the train station I felt safer. Surely the Warlock would not think to find me here? Surely this white witch of a woman would be my amulet, my delicious and juicy counter spell?

Cell took me on the train right along the coast to a place in the bush. Sitting and watching the trees crowding up to the tracks I panicked again. She held my hand, puzzled and concerned. She didn't understand me but she wasn't going to let that get in the way of what was good for me.

We got off the train and walked down a sandy track into bush. This was different forest. Not like the wet and crowded place where I grew up. It was dry and multicoloured, oddly spacious. The earth wasn't red, but pale and sandy, tussocked and rough with gravel. Instead of the countless variations of green there were ochres, greys, reds, browns, blues and blacks. There were bush flowers too. Some were odd tiny tortured shapes of very great beauty, intensely coloured pink, yellow, red, purple or white, studded amongst prickles. Others were fronded like spiders' legs or bristly as test-tube cleaners. They sparkled like stars on low lying bushes and shrubs, curled up close with dry and stunted ferns that looked miniaturised to my tropical eye. They smelled of sand and sea and faintly of honey—queerly open and fresh.

The ocean was pounding not far away. When Cell pulled me over the ridge to the top of the dunes to show me I gasped. I couldn't believe the hugeness of it, the long sliding feline power of it, purring up to caress the waiting shore and then slinking sinuous back out into mystery. It looked unreliable, private and wild. Death lived there.

I whispered, The sea. And then, Look Con, I finally made it.

—Who are you talking to? Cell asked.

—My father. He used to promise that one day I'd see the sea. He always said he'd take me surfing with him so I could see it.

—And he didn't take you?

I didn't want to answer. I couldn't tell her about myself. The stories were too strange and too incriminating. I wanted her to love me. To know nothing of me but the present and to love me. I went wheeling past her down the edge of the dunes, feckless, loose, the sand spiralling out from beneath my bare feet, uprooting sage coloured whisks of grass, eating wind. She watched me. Her face was calm when I stopped down the bottom and looked up at her, standing above me in a seagreen dress plastered to her in the faint rush of spray carried on the flap of wind.

She called out, over all the seanoise, You look so hungry, running with your mouth open. Fierce and ravenous. You look like a cat. A sphinx. Dimity the mystery woman. That's what you want isn't it? You want to be a mystery.

I quivered there below her, wind sending hair and clothes stretching ahead of me as if inclining towards her up there riding the elements like she ruled that place. Terrified that she would judge me, I nevertheless confusedly wanted to lie in the sand with her and have her kiss me with her salty mother goddess lips.

She laughed. God, don't look so lost.

Next she was naked, running for the water, grabbing my hand. Come on.

—No. I can't.

—You'll love it.

—Cats weren't made for the ocean. I can't swim.

—Just come in up to your waist. Come on!

—Please Cell no I can't please don't make me I drowned once and I really can't.

—Drowned?

— . . .

When she saw the anxiety draining my eyes she let go. Her compassion flooded me as she dived in. She was natural there. I saw her body streaming through the iridescent roll of water, as curved and plenteous as she was, watched her coiled in the waiting energies of the massive ocean, teaming her spirit with the wildness there, gasped when I saw her bodysurfing my death. Beautiful aquamarine and jade greens mottled her with foam as she poured through there, more liquid than water itself.

She came out and towelled herself. When she sat down beside me, in a little tent of towel, I could still feel the warmth coming off her body, unquenched by the ocean's chill. The sun was lowering and her face was linear and frank, gold-dipped, tenderly freckled.

—You drowned once?

— . . . Yes.

—How?

I couldn't tell her it was because my mother was giving death the option of me. Who would believe that? I didn't answer.

—There's a lot you won't talk about, she commented.

—Mmm.

—You're shivering. Come under the towel.

I got my wish when she kissed me with her salty goddess lips. It was a long and lovely moment, tart and sweet at once. Her breasts clustered against my drift-wood arm as she leaned over and smoothed the lashing hair off my cheek. Sand sifted between us.

—You've got to let go of all the shit you're carrying, she finished, explicitly.

She paused, looking at my feet. She reached out her hand, finger crooked, and said, That's a beautiful tattoo—I won't ask you what it means.

Her finger traced it from the outside end to the

centre. I felt unbelievably caressed and connected. Did she find me in that moment? Months of hiding later I don't know anymore, especially with all the changes and the bitterness. I think she did find me though. That instant was like being in the womb. Or like being in the womb should be, when you are wanted. Just then, the spiral serpent became a lovely cord which bound me to her. And the wonder was, she let herself be bound.

Back at the office Cell asked me, How did you end up here?

I blinked. I didn't answer.

—You haven't worked out your story yet, is that it?

Wounded. It's just that I can't explain. It doesn't feel real. You might not believe me.

Cell was tactful. You got hurt in some way?

—I've been very sick, and I've nearly died, more than once.

—Someone abused you?

—A man wanted to marry me, but I couldn't do it. He wanted to change everything about me. He changed . . . most things. I've been an unwanted child, an unrequited lover, a demon and a freak. I've been Frankenstein's monster. I've been Barbie. I was almost a bride. But I never did anything properly. I always fell short somewhere.

Cell never even questioned the probability of my words. She simply took my two shoulders and made the invitation that changed her life.

—Look, why don't you come home with me and stay at my place tonight? There's room.

And all of a sudden she'd sealed her fate. And mine too. It was a fate that had already taken shape, for from the moment that I opened the door which separated us, Cell and I were connected. It is not untrue to say that we had become sisters in a destiny. If I had not been so confused and hunted I might have stopped to parry Morgan on that one. I might have asserted my right to protect someone from the curse which dogged me. But I was too desperate and panic-stricken. I needed Cell and her unity. So when she asked me to stay I didn't think twice. I accepted her blessing.

At three o'clock that morning we come sidling through the darkened laminex. Our two live bodies slip through the glossed surfaces, the panelled glass and stainless steel, plummet to ground in the lift. Holding hands, we step into the street. Cool breezes scarf around us, light bows and warps from street fittings, shops and offices, and there is the snarling looping flare of car headlights. Watch the night expand and contract, watch the currents tearing through the huge life that is a city, watch the refuse and the glittering goods.

Watch Cell—she creams her pacific way through all this. The cluttered claustrophobia and all the little traps part to allow her passage. And watch me, clinging to her warm fingers, just attached to the serenely directed force that is Cell, bobbing in her big and beautiful wake!

While you're watching me you will notice that I glance right and left. I watch every crevice and every corner. When a pigeon ruffles my ear in flight I cringe and stammer, N-n-no.

In my world there are pterodactyl forces of surveillance which swoop and skite when they go back to the master to report that they've found me, they've tracked me down. There are arms which shoot out of darkened doorways and drag me in there. There are caves everywhere which link up to Morgan's secret places. Reality is labyrinthine, and every place flaunts its connection with danger. There is terror in the sky, and the pavements wait to open up beneath me.

And even so there is Cell, singing snatches of sea shanties as she kicks a can and makes it skip over two separate crevices in the pavement, swinging both her arms and sending me twirling back and forth to her breathing intimate tunes. There are moaning clucking happy sounds that she makes—odd sighs and giggles and whooshing whispers when she points out something she is looking at. She is a magnificent distraction. She keeps me on course, steers me easily through the maze.

We come then to the docks. The sight of the bony back of wharf hunched over the hiss of harbour waters is frightening. Not to Cell, she trips over the planks as if they are piano keys and stirs more songs from them. She creaks and crackles, the water underneath slaps and tickles and strokes. They know one another.

But I don't know the water. I want my feet on dry land. I don't want to trip along the vertebrae of the wharf as she does. I know that wharf might just as well buck me off and tip me into the drink. Standing dwarfed, shadowed at the place where the gutter butts up against the invitation of wharf back, I watch Cell reeling gracefully along its whole length, absorbed in play. I will not set foot on the wharf.

When she reaches the end she stops. She's a long way away. Her hands are beckoning as she calls me. Come on Dimity, come on.

It's a temptation! She is there above the seeming quiet waves, smiling the seductress smile, hooking me into the magic of her charisma and the protection it appears to offer, winding me towards her like you wind the caught fish. The fish resists and fights in spangled terrors. Red blood rushes from its gashes and when you bring it in you are forced to see those red flowers again.

—Come on!

She is insistent, doesn't understand the paralysis of childhood fear. If my death lives in the water, frogged out like a diver but with no time limit on his tanks, how can she be other than siren, beckoning me to perform the impossible and walk on water, cajoling me to dive toward her false bosom and give away my learned fears, promising euphoria and boundless senseless selfless pleasure?

Her patience has run out and she comes pelting down the wharf, every plank pounded like a drum. It's a death roll. Sure enough she's rolled me. She's caught me up in a role reversal, dived on *me* now that she's sick of waiting for me to dive on her. She leaps right up and envelops me. Gulp and I am gone, pressed against the heaving solidity of her chest, with her ribs all around me and her arms encircling while she takes her captive down the bony back of the wharf and to the boat.

On board.

If my mad mother's ghost had been able to make herself heard at this point, I know she would have had something to say about this. She would have seen it not only as a joke, but as a riddle:

When a whale, swimming large off the coast of Australia, sees a boat floating above it, what does it see?

A leaf rimmed in silver, rocked lightly but rigid?

A half-being?

The belly perhaps of some odd simulacrum, a whale Frankenstein skilfully assembled by humans?

Maybe the whale calls out in greeting, fills the noisy thick ocean with clicks and squeaks and moans, and is surprised to hear from this incomplete being only the slap and bubble of waters against it.

And when Cell, floating free in the fluid waters of her own consciousness, spots the stick-legged figure of Dimity paddling stiffly (and a shade desperately) on the surface of her mind, does she stretch out towards her in compassion, or does she dive deep because she feels the danger vibe pulsing through her element?

She did the first thing. Even though everyone she knew counselled her against adopting strays and advised her not to get stuck being a do-good twit.

Morgan's laugh, had she been able to enjoy it, would have pealed right out, as loudly as if she'd been alive.

5 The Vessel

It wasn't so bad. In fact it was wonderful. Inside the boat was all wood and smooth surfaces. Everything was streamlined. There was a snugness to it—each edge closely planed to nudge the next, each line tapering neatly into others, each contour moulded close to another. The effect integrated, enclosed, efficient.

I had a fold-down bunk outside the cabin where Cell slept. Deep in night when she'd returned from the office, I lay there, imagining her stretched out like a princess on her bed just the other side of the panels, the sigh of her acquiescent tranquil breath brushing the ceiling, painting her quiet and fulfilled dreams there like delicate and fanciful murals. Light radiated out of her.

For the first time ever, I felt safe in my bed. In our little pod, tethered to the twisting grainy backbone of our wharf, we swayed and rocked to rhythms pulsing from all over the world and carried in water. Cradled there, I slept dreamless sleep, the drenching quiet sleep of peace.

There was work for me there. Cell offered to supply me with food if I would do some of the maintenance. Only a few hours a day. The boat was like a child—it required constant tending. I sat in the rushing sunlight on deck, painstakingly taking apart the brass fittings one by one, polishing them until they blinded me, then reassembling them. I sanded and varnished, scraped and painted, swept and sponged, scrubbed, wiped, dusted. The boat became my constant concern, the recipient of a beautiful new me that knew how to care for something and was cared for in return. I had an esoteric knowledge of knots, acquired during my days at the freak show. There were a lot of uses for knots in a temporary environment of tents and caravans, groundsheets, trapezes, hidden strings, leashes. There were also a lot of uses for knots on the boat. I constantly astonished Cell with this or that extraordinary new convolution of rope, the manifold purposes it could serve. All of a sudden, I was the bearer of knowledge coveted by another.

Over the period that I lived with Cell I got brown from living on the deck. My hair took on a sunbleached lustre and the panic receded in my eyes. I was still scrawny, but I began to look, after my own fashion, healthy.

Look at it from my perspective—living on the edge of the land as we did, insulated by water, we were the furthest we could possibly be from the three deaths remaining. Those deaths were by fire, except for the one which was by poison. The deaths by drowning were finished now, part of my past. So the water was safe—it didn't have it in for me. And for the first time in ages I felt a clear pulse towards the idea of living. Now that my life went beyond base survival and began to embrace leisure, pleasure, and tranquillity, I didn't want to let go of it. My desire to survive framed itself in more than brute instinct and began to finesse itself. For the first time the possibility of happiness, love, and even success crept in and laced its edges.

I had even stopped expecting Lock and Morgan to arrive at any moment. I still feared them though. Deep in me there was a nagging unstill space where Morgan crouched, occasionally stretching and pawing her confinement, flexing her confidence in her own destructive powers. I suppressed her, barred the doors against her and Lock. Battened down the hatches. Felt them writhing, plotting.

There was one recognised shade on my happiness. That was that Cell wanted us to put to sea in the boat. She wanted to show me what it would be like out on the ocean where we couldn't see the land at all. She spent many hours trying to persuade me to cast off. Though I loved and trusted her and felt safe on the boat where it rested tied up to the wharf, I could not yet love and trust the ocean enough to ride its untrammeled curves. It was as if all the many fears which made up my consciousness had been anchored onto this one fear, transmuted into one big remaining fear that could not be superseded. A fear quite immune to happiness and security. The kind of big irrational fear that usually means secret knowledge. I knew the ocean was death's place. And even though I knew I couldn't die now by sea, I still could not trust. I couldn't risk Cell out there. She was vulnerable in her fearlessness. Though the ocean was her element this was not protection against the pathology of what I knew to be my native surrounds. I didn't want to lose her.

6 THE VOICE

I told you that I thought Cell was the woman who had everything. One of the best things that she had was Sly. I fell in love with Sly's voice. It wasn't that I wanted the body of Cell's lover. Why would I, when I had Cell's body? I desired only his voice. It was a voice that I wanted draped around me at night like mosquito netting. I wanted to stay in the web of it and keep the buzzing nothings out of my head, where they swarmed unchecked some nights and brought me out in welts.

Sly had the voice that most radio announcers have, laced with superficiality, but with him it was sincere and radiantly warm like sun rays. It was a voice that irresistibly attracted others, like me. A voice like chocolate. Addictive. Was this how he had attracted someone as magnificent as Cell?

I had been so quiet for so long that an observer might have thought that the spiral serpent's function had long changed. Anyone might have thought that I'd lost my powers, that the lyrebird had gone down in the fire. But as you've seen, I am a phoenix, and it takes a lot to kill me, or any part of me. Even though the Warlock had paralysed me I had the coil of potency still within me.

And as I told you before, it took the lure of another voice to bring it out. The voice was Sly's.

The first time I heard his voice on the answering machine my heart groaned. I was hooked. Cell told me that he worked on national radio. For the last month he had been broadcasting out of Alice Springs. He was doing a series of programs, rotating his base around Australia's major cities. I listened to him every weeknight, from ten until two in the morning. Cell would be out at the office. I'd curl up on the couch and wait for him to begin. With all the lights out I could imagine that he was there beside me, talking right into my ear. Over and over again he'd tell me it would all be okay.

That's how I came to spend the days with Cell, and the nights with her lover. They became the two forces which structured my life. On the one hand Cell, whom I wanted to love me as a sister. No, not just that. I also wanted her to love me as a child. She was like the Madonna, holding out this wonderful radiant promise of pure unconditional love. In my imagination I saw her with a shell of light around her, smiling and extending a hand from the blue centre of her tranquil self.

That wasn't the whole of it though. On the other hand there was Sly, God to Cell's Madonna. Inaccessible, vast, inscrutable. The consciousness who could set up the world in six days just by talking about it. I knew my world could do with some work, and I had him earmarked for the reconstruction.

The thing which started me back with the spiral serpent was talkback. I hadn't called the serpent up since the night when I'd murdered Antonio Houdini Grieg. I'd kept it bottled up, corked and quiet. Since that night, I'd often looked at my tattoo and thought about it, the coiled power waiting for a chance to be expressed, getting ready to weave and sway in the vacuous centre of my world, and strike out of it at the uninterpretable clutter which fringed it. Frankly, I was afraid to let it loose. It knew this. I could feel its sinuous length twisting restlessly on nights when the silence was so heavy I felt pinioned by it. But I denied it, because I was afraid.

When Sly started talkback I listened as if my life depended upon it. I suppose it did, in a way. Because I'd decided that his voice was the tightrope to which I must peg my disorderly lot. So I hung there, avid. Until one night he hosted the talkback on test-tube babies. The spiral serpent whiplashed and got loose. Of course it was Morgan who'd prised the trapdoor, worrying and teasing until that frenzied power had to strike. She knew that if she could only badger it into a resurgence, she would have started something. However benign the beginnings of a deception, she trusted herself to nurture them into a fullblown and poisonous charade. This was her expertise, and I was little more than the puppet. Or so I tell myself, wanting to forget that the only truly erotic reaction I ever had in my life was to the voice of Sly. Still now I deny that my one talent, my ventriloquism, had finally found its raison d'être. I don't remember picking up the phone, but suddenly I was talking to him. He was asking me to turn my radio off so that the static noises would stop. I turned it off.

I told him I was a test-tube baby.

—There aren't an awful lot of you out there, are there? Do you feel something of a rarity?

—Yes. But sometimes when I'm unhappy I feel like a freak. It's hard to know that you came about because of technology. Like you're an experiment, or something. It's . . . forced, do you see what I mean?

—So you feel that the way you were conceived has formed your sense of self in a negative way?

—Yes. It's not real, not real like sex is real. I'm unnatural. A product.

—That's really interesting. But what about the fact that your parents must have truly wanted you in order to make it through that whole process of IVF? Surely that's a comfort to know that you are one of the most planned and wanted children to have ever been born?

—Yes. But that's their obsession. And the doctor's. Children are made out of something . . . is it love? God, I don't know, desire? It's chance, as much as anything else. But not . . . obsession. Not bloodymindedness. Sometimes I feel like I'm living a dream—my mother's nightmare. As if I started out as her fantasy, but something went wrong and it became a nightmare. I didn't turn out to be the baby she wanted.

—But you're here now, and for that you've got to be thankful, eh? Thanks a lot for your contribution to tonight's discussion; let's move on now and hear what Greg has to say.

He hung up on me.

It got so that whenever he did talkback I took on

one of my own stray voices and called him. I'd use a different name every time. But I'd take every opportunity to speak to him, to try and make contact. But just like that first night, he always evaded me. He always stopped me from really touching the velvet edge of the voice. As if it was his cloak, and he'd whip it out from under me as I tried to close my fingers over its hem. As I revealed myself, he shut me out. In the end, he always hung up on me.

Morgan whispered in my ear. She was getting very restless in there. Caged in the ribbed span of the new me, she began to rake her fingers along the striations from the inside, tickling from within. She told me to do what I did. It was always Morgan who set me up for the big ones.

It started out with her telling me to listen in on the extension when Cell took calls from Sly. I remarked my crippling jealousy at their intimacy. I learned to control this by pretending that I was Cell as I listened, and that his words were really meant for me. I was expert at these sorts of games. After all, I'd been playing them most of my life.

Then Morgan pushed me that step further. She prompted me, once I'd perfected the trick of being Cell, to call his answering machine and leave messages for him, using Cell's voice. I imagined him walking into his office in a cloud of words just said, a beautiful thick swathe wrapped about him like a halo, responding to my little flashing red light, the beacon I'd put out there for him, pressing the button to listen to me.

—Hi sweetheart, it's me. I hope you're having a gorgeous night. I just called to say I absolutely adore you and wish you were here. Bye now.

Back in the old days I would have had someone to talk to about the way I was feeling about that voice. I would have been able to pick up Barbarella, send the spiral serpent rocketing up the ladder and across the deck, right down to the end of the rickety grey wharf, and we could have gossiped the night away until Cell got back, Barbarella bitching and criticising and undermining me. At least I would have had someone to talk to. If I hadn't been cursed, in this case with an obsession for a man who was the beloved of the one woman who had ever dared to be my friend, perhaps I could have replaced that truant Barbarella with Cell. Maybe we two could have sat up on the deck in the small hours, our feet dangling over the side and the whole world in love with us, and giggled about my infantile loves and petty deceptions. We could have shared it. But how could we ever do that, when the thread of my own destruction had led me to this warped eros for Cell's boyfriend's voice?

No, now there was only Morgan, getting louder, nagging away in the back of my head, filling it with incantations and her black and ugly jokes. She was working her way loose. Sure enough, the next week I opened the hold to get supplies, and I quailed to see her eucalypt form come twisting and streaming from the hole like the smoke of a bad genie. Her long brown limbs branched and gnarled against the air and hanging off them like the strips of bark from a gum tree were the charred tatters of her widow's weeds, black satin besmirched by ash and cinders. Her brow was deformed with rage and the stress of pleasant seeming given the factors ranged against her—it is hard to look benign when you have a frown hacked into your forehead like an axe mark, and all your skin is wealed and smeared in ash. She held her arms above her head and writhed as if in a gale, pinioning me with her black and steadfast crazy eyes.

—You know what to do now, don't you?

—Shut up Morgan. The volcano ate you. You can't talk any more. Your tongue got burned out and you're dead dead dead. Go away.

—He is your love, your destiny. Just as I am, you moronic child. And it will be so easy to get him, because all you have to do is pick up the phone.

—What do you mean?

—I mean that you can be her voice.

—Whose voice?

—Hers. The fat lady.

—She *is not* fat.

—You miss the point, my dim one. Always missing the point, that's you.

When Morgan grinned her teeth looked like splinters. Truly, she was carnivorous. She continued. Once you've got him where you want him, you can have him.

—Have him?

—The seduction is yours. The prize will be won. Yours will be the little ear where he squirts all those puffed up pretentious words you love to hear. And so for the rest of you. Isn't it funny that, puny froggy thing that you are, it appears that you have your very own appeal? You are going to bed that bullfrog.

I was horrified. Her words were treacherous, blasphemous. I was blinded with anger and a fear that was the more potent for being a premonition and I spat at her, Shut up Morgan. You're a sati. Dead and burnt and buried. All at once. I can't hear you—that's how dead you are.

Morgan opened her bloodless lips, revealing once more those splinter teeth, but before she could speak I started wailing to drown her out. Morgan though considered her mission complete, and she cackled as she shrank back into the hold. Even though I was screaming, I did hear her final words as I fastened the hatch with tremoring hands, You can't bury *me*.

I cried myself to sleep because Morgan made me so scared I wished I could die but couldn't see how to die another three deaths quick enough to stop me from enacting the curse. Poison was easy enough but two deaths by fire? Even my runtling soul, schooled to treat dying as part of life, could see that that wasn't going to be easy.

Morgan had perceived my naked desire for Sly's voice. She knew at once that this was her weapon. She worked on it until one day my desire did get the better of me and caused me to reel Cell's voice in off the backbone of the spiral serpent and throw it to Sly like a prize catch.

That night, I lay for a very long time on the couch in the lounge room, savouring the idea of speaking to him. He had hung up on me countless times, cut me off. But I was going to make him see a conversation through. Little me with my wispy hair and frightened eyes had nevertheless strands of iron wire trussing up my weak little will and making it strong enough to triumph even over him, a muscular man with murderously powerful vocal chords. Remarkable but true: my whining, shy, vulnerable voice could contrive to bind his chords, tie him to a lie of my own devising and tease him with it until he couldn't remember what was true any more. That stuff is easy.

From my position on the bench below deck I could see the deck and a wedge of sky. There was no moon and despite the city glow the sky was packed with stars—just so many more glares from the universe. I stared them out. It went like this.

My left hand slides up the panelling and onto the jack where the mobile phone clings, suspended. Legs are sliding too, one over the other, and back is coiled while tongue comes out once or twice to lick lips. These are dry and wrinkling because I am parched for this. It's a while now that I have waited. But I won't wait more.

So I am unhooking the phone, fingering the mouthpiece and stroking the pad of numbers into my coil, and listening while my long nails get caught up in the cord as I stretch and release, stretch and release and Sly is answering my scratching at his door, oblivious to the unfurling of my spiral serpent.

—Hello?

—Hello Sly.

—Cell. Hi. Nice to hear your voice.

Nice is bland. Far from it for me—I am hallucinating huge pink and orange hibiscus flowers floating lurid. His voice has me losing my mind. I have to focus. I say, I've been thinking about you.

—Yeah? What have you been thinking?

Where does it come from? I don't know. It comes.

—I want us to have a baby, Sly.

A very strange, long silence. It is like having a life-support system cut off but not dying straight away. As if someone has decreed that you must truly experience the deprivation before it kills you. Then the voice again, swelling up and wrapping me in a sumptuous purple place where I am quailing and too happy to think straight.

—Have you been drinking Cell? Are you down? Cell, don't torture yourself, okay?

Even in my euphoria, my intoxicated wallowing in the lap of his power, I recognise a curiosity and my cleverness cannot let it go. There is a little crackling, a laddering of the smooth timbres as I climb out with just a bit of craft and flare out another Cell.

—Why Sly? Why not a baby?

—Cell, darling, you know why not. You've had every test under the bloody sun and basically life's a bitch and you're never going to have any kids and I'm fucking sorry okay but I love you more than life itself and I promise you that this is never ever going to matter to me and you will never hurt about it because of me.

Please, Cell, just let it go, will you? Don't do it to yourself. You've been through it enough now.

—Sly, I'm sorry.

—That's okay. Let's just forget we had this conversation, alright? When I speak to you next it will be like we never talked about this again. Alright?

—Alright.

—I've got to go now, Cell. I'm on in two minutes. Take care of yourself.

—Yes.

—Bye.

—Bye.

The phone is slipping into its resting place, languorous. I am loose and trying to come down. I am high. Just from speaking to him. But there's more: there's information. Something is new in my mind.

Looking back on this scene now, don't you wonder about my instinct? How I could touch the only nerve worth touching, and find it a common one? Isn't it a potent argument for destiny? When a woman is surviving by her wits in the middle of a nightmare, but the nightmare has been conceived without an exit point, even that woman's cleverness can only lead deeper into the fear. Because there is no way out.

7 Lashed Together

I've explained that Cell was fearless. She had good reason to be, because she was the closest thing I'd ever met to a goddess. She tested everything. She did it without thinking mostly. But when her experiments were premeditated she was stunning.

You've been tied up there for a long time, listening. You've had my voice in your ears. You've seen me victimised, but just then you saw me sin. You would have judged me, no doubt. But you have the webbed mouth of an entombed mummy, and you've been forced to stay put, refused the right to pass comment. I propose to you that I was not malicious, but simply continuing to play out my destiny. And it's not Cell's fault, but somehow her destiny is knotted securely into mine. She can't help it. Nor can I. But just as you sit there, bound somehow in this tale of mine, we two embarked together on a common voyage where we were inextricably and fatefully entwined. So before you blame me, before you join in on the hating of me, see what happened next.

One day, when the sun stroked the world into one long radiant exclamation of pleasure, I heard a strange sound. It was a purring feline sound that went through the entire boat. Curled up in my bunk, catnapping and quiet, I dozed at first on the edges of the sound. Until I surfaced in the warm and fuggy air, and saw the land outside scrolling past like cinema.

Cell had started the engine. While I slept, she had cast loose the knots which tethered us to our parent wharf, and we were cruising out of the harbour.

I ran upstairs. I was speechless with fear.

Cell in the wheelhouse, grinning into the saltier and saltier air, angelic and adventurous. I found a word.

—Shit!

—Don't overreact. I decided it was time we dealt with that last fear of yours. I know you can take it. Look—it's the open ocean. Only another couple of hours and we won't see land. You'll love it.

I didn't love it. I knew it was a disaster. The whole time that we steamed out into the flat expanse of that sea I spent crouched inside the wheelhouse, ignoring Cell's encouraging words, refusing to look. I'd seen the bland impenetrable grey blue of the surface, looking so safe, when I'd first rushed into the wheelhouse, riding my own hysteria. And I'd seen in that the surface that it would become.

Sure enough I perceived the wind long before Cell noticed it from the wheel, where she was busy, navigating competently and intermittently crowing with delight at the sight of the sea. I felt the jaws of that wind come masked to us, and I saw the mask parting and heard the gnashing, ever so soft, just as it began. When the wailing started I was ready. It was as I expected, cut with trembling groans of thunder. There was no need to get up—

through the windows from where I crouched splaylegged on the floor, I could see the warrior clouds streaming from the east, their black helmets steeling what was left of the sunlight into skewering arrows as they advanced in formation, hurly-burly, icy cold, against the warm air that was left around us. No need to get up to see what all this was doing to the ocean, diced under the blades of those clouds, ragged and luminously blue in the cracks fired by sun swords and shot lightning.

Cell's harmony just creased as she realised the coming storm was serious. Still she had no real understanding of what it was to fear. That would come though. Frowning, she changed course.

The universe growled and suddenly, with the force of a panther springing from ambush, the storm caught us up and the battering began. It was a small boat and the pounding of the rain upon it was utterly deafening. I saw Cell holding the wheel, strobed in lightning. Her movements were broken up, segmented into tiny submovements. She looked unreal, robotic. In the dreadful light she looked horrifyingly like Morgan. Her eyes were pitted. She tossed me a life-jacket.

—Here, put that on if you're scared.

I didn't know how. It took me a long time to work it out. In that time the storm intensified still further. Clutching the pitching floor I surrendered to tears. While I sobbed hopelessly Cell busied herself securing everything. The dreadful racking motion dominated all my thought and I puked out my queasy horrified guts on the carpet at her feet. Just as I did so, there was a dull wrenching sound at the glass of the wheelhouse door. The pane crazed.

—It's the fucking clothes-line come loose. Should never have extras like that on a boat. Got to tie it down.

The clothes-line was attached at either end by a heavy metal hook. One end had come unscrewed, and the force of the winds was trailing the whole line, with Cell's swimsuit and bra and two of my t-shirts still amazingly pegged on, and whirling it in air, bringing it whipping against the side of the boat, the windows, whatever chaotic place it was borne.

Bashing ocean noise as Cell slid the door open and disappeared into the meshing bruised air outside. In a few moments she came back in.

—Can't hold it. I'm sorry mate but you're going to have to come out there and help me fasten it. Or cut it off. I'm not sure yet which is best.

She was sympathetic but firm. Whimpering, I knew I'd have to obey.

—Come on. Look—I'll tie you onto the railing by your life-jacket. That'll make you feel more secure, won't it? We've got to move fast—that hook could do more damage than just breaking the glass. We don't want the bloody thing carving into the hull.

Cell climbed out and knotted me fast to the railing. She pulled me out the door and onto the deck. She shouted, watch out for that line. Could come at you any time. Listen if I call out, and get ready to duck. Do what I say.

The line came writhing through air, snaking

towards me with a snarl tempered by the frantic snicker of wet clothes in gale force winds. I didn't need Cell's imperative—DUCK! and was flat to the deck before she even opened her mouth. Jumped up again to see a crash of white water shaped like a fist with claws slam onto the deck between me and Cell. There was an anguishing pitch and shudder and a squeal of timber. When the air cleared I made out Cell, struggling with one end of the line, looking absurdly like a snake charmer in crisis. She shrieked—Hold this! and I grasped the body of the python, flexing with awesome power in my weak fingers. One of the t-shirts plastered my desperate face and I didn't see but felt the line lose its mooring and channel slack out of my grasp. Realised that Cell had got it loose and heard her say—Let go. Felt the whole contraption yanked up into the sky with me on the end of it, obeying just in time and opening my eyes to see a phantasmagorical flight of two t-shirts, a bra and a swimsuit, flapping like ill-assorted wings so that the snake became airborne, sailing out into the black and blue horizon, undulating briefly in a wonder of loops lassoing and then spiralling down to the—

Yes to the sea! Which I'd avoided looking at until now. But trained there, trailing the suicidal flightpath of that freed line, my gaze was quashed in the stacking tumble of waves and the brutal thundrous talk of the angry angry sea.

It was at precisely that moment that the boat plunged nauseatingly into a cavernous grave of a trough and Cell went overboard.

I loved Cell. I still love her more than anyone else I ever knew. That's why I only paused for a split second before I entrusted myself to the life-jacket and the line and jumped after her.

You might scoff. You might remind yourself in your numbed incommunicado world that I knew there were no more deaths by water. That I'd dared the unscheduled deaths before and won, that I knew the water would spare me because this was not my appointed ending. Scoff all you like, if you can manage it through those stitches. But give yourself pause and imagine what it costs a cat to jump into a bath. Then scale that up and try to imagine what it cost me to cast my body into that seething troubled vat of ocean. A person who has drowned already whilst only a baby! I don't ask you to admire me, or call me brave. I don't want decorations or recognition. I just want this information stored for later. It's proof. Proof that I truly truly loved Cell and that my love of her was so great it could even conquer a malevolent fear.

So once again in my bizarre and difficult life I was airborne. I felt myself thrust up in the wounded rattled air, riddled by rain bullets, the old rag doll body flapping briefly against its line in the black and blue world and smacking soundly, painfully against the rearing back of the sea. The sea bucked me, tossed me roughly with asphyxiating jerks on my line. But my mouth was clear and I had it open and ready. When I came up onto the crest I scanned for Cell. Couldn't see her, swooped down again into shaded tomb of trough, coughed at the water in my mouth, rose again screaming her name but still no sign of her so down once more into the inevitable curve. On and on until finally I did see her. And her companion.

Yes. Death was there again, all togged out in the diver's suit, surfing a pinnacled wave that threatened to crush the bobbing body of Cell.

But Cell couldn't see that. She wasn't interested in death. She didn't believe in death. She saw me though. Grinned her determination. With deliberate strokes she urged against the ocean. No panic, just will. That was Cell. I saw death nosedive on the shredding laced crest of the wave and get dumped.

Cell's breath raked my hand as I held it out to her when she got close enough. She grasped it and we were connected. The two of us connected in the heavy fathoms of water, still linked to our battered boat. We were crying.

—You silly . . . she murmured, her exhaustion only now shadowing her spear of will. I can't believe you jumped in.

Entwined there, we breathed (yinyang) together. My rubber-band arms were around her solid streamlined torso, my flyaway body was pinging against her like a kite in wind. The skin of our faces slimed over with tears and spray. We were like one being. Siamese twins who shared the same heart.

As if in honour of this peculiar birth, everything stilled. The passing storm gave us a backhanded spattering of the gentlest rain. It was like a blessing. That's the hypocrisy of ocean. Our upturned faces, pallid as two poached eggs, spotted with droplets and with crystallised salt hardened along our lashes, were shadowed by the side of the boat looming above us. Merciful, that long creamy white shape, gentle as a whale.

Cell was able to haul herself up along the line. She pulled me up after her. She wouldn't let me lie on the deck, forced me inside to a hot shower, blankets, brandy. The boat was undamaged. We were able to start heading home.

After that, we both knew that we'd never be apart again. We were lashed together in those minutes. We would be lashed together for the rest of our lives.

That was the night that Cell and I generated the idea. When we got back to the wharf and tied up, Cell pulled me into her bed for warmth and we clung together there.

She whispered her confession.

—I have to tell you something.

—Mmm?

—I haven't told anyone else this. Only Sly. But I can't ever have children.

—I know.

In the darkness I could sense her surprise, almost instantaneously quenched by her acceptance. There could be no secrets between us. Not after everything that had happened. It seemed right to her that I should intuit her best kept secrets.

—But you *can* have children. Look—my body is your body.

She understood right away. In the euphoria of my

having saved Cell's life, we saw a radiant future, and the end of Cell's childlessness. We had already proved that we were two parts of the same body—there was no reason why I couldn't have a child for Cell.

We hugged close. Our hearts were synchronised.

Part Five

THE BIG SCREEN

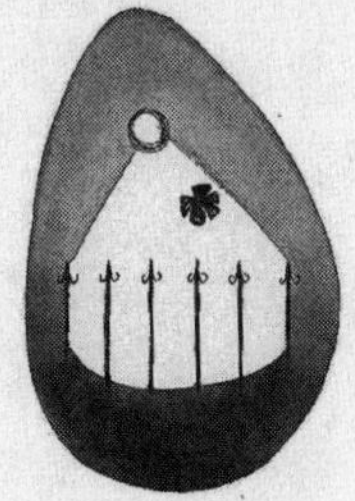

1 A THIRD

We slept until the next day. My face tickled in the hot roil of Cell's hair, which I didn't brush off because it was so comforting. I pressed my chin into her shoulder.

There was a tower going up over our bed, a tower ascending. From its viewfinding pinnacle there was scrutiny. The air vibrated with surprise and something else. Jealousy? In the shadow of this tower we both murmured restlessly, nudged muddled thoughts into the shaded periphery of sleep, stirred and opened our eyes.

To see a man looking down on our bed.

I sat up immediately. I could feel the compelling eye of Lock upon me. The man his messenger. Before I could scream Cell's right hand shot out and seized him, toppling him into our bed, collapsing him on top of her. Then she was kissing him. She had her passionate tongue against his teeth and I could see her hands move swift like waves over his shoulders and down, rolling into the small of his back and cresting his buttocks in a powerful eddying caress.

What could he do but surrender?

Of course it was Sly.

Watching them was like being at the movies. They were larger than life and abundant with happy endings.

Watching them, I longed to be part of what they had. I wanted to be their child. Or I wanted to have their child. Either way I wanted to be the third. I only wanted to be integrated into the radiant fabric of their world, to stay with them and be their third, right up to the happy ending. Everything happened because of that.

With Sly back, the tenor of my happiness changed. I was still happy. Here after all I was cupped in a beautiful world where I had two reference points on tap—Cell's body and Sly's voice.

It was true that his voice still held me. I still yearned to hear him. It was funny; having him in front of me wasn't the same. It turned out that I didn't need to see him. I discovered that I liked best the darkened room, and his voice on the radio when he did his usual nightshift. I liked to be netted in his voice, to swing in it like a hammock. I didn't need his physical presence. Because Sly turned out to be imposing but somehow flat in person. Remote, panoramic, inaccessible, he was a screen animated totally by the wonder spirit of his vocal chords. It was only through interaction with Cell that he achieved three dimensionality. She gave him physicality and form. It seemed that he loved her for the same reasons I did, if not with the same desperation.

Sly wanted me to have the baby. He had always wanted a third. He wanted it as insurance, so that the issue of childlessness would never come between him and Cell in the future. Also, Sly fundamentally didn't see why anything in life should be denied him. It never had, up until now. So he was determined to stamp out this first little diversion from his path before any kind of pattern set in. He didn't see any problem with using a surrogate mother, just as long as he didn't have to sleep with her and as long as there was some kind of contractual and financial understanding firmly stitched up.

But he didn't really want it to be me. I could see that when he looked at me. I could see the thoughts scrolling through his eyes. It always started with him sizing me up, wondering how the hell my stringy legs could hold up a pregnancy. Scrutinising my concave gut, incredulous of any sign of change there. Assessing my tits—asking himself were they too puny to nourish Cell's and his child? It ended up with him peering unfathomably into my eyes and doubting that such fear and vulnerability could be receptive. How could a new life graft itself onto such an impoverished sprig as this? If children are made of love, how could this body, that looked as if it had never ever been loved, play host?

Maybe, he wondered, they should look for someone else to do the job. But who else would take it on? He was an opportunist, and he knew a tough brief when he saw one. He realised that there weren't many people like me out there—no money, no friends or family, no goals or aspirations, adoring of Cell and admiring of him. Young, presumably fertile. I was alone enough for the whole thing to be kept secret, dependent enough to need the money they could offer, devoted enough for them to control me.

He knew he'd be mad to give up this one chance,

the chance of a lifetime with Cell, and resigned himself to my imperfections. No, not imperfections, not blemishes, but a different problem altogether; really it was lack. Something missing. He turned a blind eye to what wasn't there. The *if onlys* kept coming though: if only I was someone more balanced, stronger, saner, more beautiful, more intelligent, more like Cell . . . the list went on.

Sly wasn't to know that I had inherited something more than Morgan's dark eyes and hair, more than her lean dark body. He didn't know about the curse, patterned into my being as surely as if it was coded into my DNA.

So before anyone had really understood the implications, our strange relationship was underway. I began, using a syringe, to work on creating the third.

Look at the ectoplasmic fluid in the syringe! It's a ghost of a child to come. A phantom child.

I start thinking of part lives. Lives lived sectionally, unconventionally. I remember the dolls. Some frozen in babyhood, others atrophied in childhood, still others rigidly adolescent. Culminating of course in those dolls that circumvented the whole life cycle and were created woman. No one made old dolls. This curious thought sidetracks me for a moment before I break it off to speak aloud to my lost childhood friend.

—Barbarella, you never had a childhood. You graduated straightaway to a woman's body. But you were never made to be a vessel. You hardliner.

Barbarella's hard lines would have refused, right from the very beginning. But somehow I've been roped in. I said I'd give motherhood a go. Even if it's for someone else.

And look, I give it my best shot: I say a prayer as I hold the syringe up and look close at the future. It's hard to believe that this liquid can shape the future. It looks so pale and bland, so thin and paltry. A nonevent.

I'm shooting up. I see the curves of Cell and I feel myself her vessel. Sly's voice in my ears, I am feeding my addiction. My inner thighs are sticky. I look down and only see the gloss upon them. No flowers. Just as well.

It wasn't as easy as we'd thought it would be. I suppose we all thought I'd conceive straight away. That we'd set off at once on the clear trail to a finished product, our joint offspring. That it would all happen like it did in the movies. I hadn't even stopped to think that Morgan would have a say in things.

One month passed. Then another. Finally three months went past. Still I didn't conceive. There started to be some small unavowed level of tension.

Every month Sly asked me, Well?

And I told him, Not yet.

I'd look disappointed. He'd be distant. Really he didn't care how I felt. He just wished I'd conceive so he could stop wanking into jars. He felt like the sacrificial cow, milking himself dry for two high priestesses. And he was worried. Hand in his pants all the time, squeezing that poor udder for more of the vital juices and getting no results, he was starting to wonder if perhaps *he* was a dud.

He started to work on Cell. He was starting to want me out. I overheard him talking to Cell in bed one night. Their voices seeped muted through the panelling.

—She's a stray. She's got that thin stricken look that they get when they've been surviving by the skin of their teeth for a long time.

—Yeah. But don't hold that against her. It's not her fault if she's had a hard life, never enough love. She's beautiful too.

—Beautiful?

—Yeah. Those perfect cheekbones and nose, the huge dark eyes and the slightness of her. Like a fairy. Some skinny cheeky spirit come slinking out of the gum trees, born out of mist and spring rains, dusted with wildflowers. Lost in the city and looking for a home. When I found her she had an amnesiac quality, as if the whole world was strange to her. Crazy beauty—like a vagabond or a dirty child. Or a lunatic. I fell for it. You can't see it?

—No.

Sly argued that Cell was mothering me, using me as a replacement for the child she'd never had. He was determined not to play daddy. He'd save that up for his real baby. Only then would he play daddy. He asked her how long I was going to stay, lectured her about taking in strays, and told her that if she was going to start adopting street kids to fill the gaps he'd have to argue for them applying to start the IVF program. He wasn't jealous of me—he was too confident for that. But he didn't like me being around because he considered me low grade. He doubted that I could pull it off and give them a baby. He argued that they should set a limit, decide a point where they stopped the arrangement. They could always look for someone else.

—No. There's no one else.

—Surely . . .

—No. She's special. She saved my life. She's part of me. She's the only one who can do this. I couldn't let just anyone into my life like this. There's got to be a bond.

I recognised in Sly an opponent. I realised that he would force me out if I failed. That would be a disaster. I wanted his voice and her body. The two of them completed my world, defined it and gave it reason. What was one without the other? I couldn't imagine being lost once more on the outside, back there where I didn't have her to shape the competition of the voices into the unity which must have pre-existed them, or him to command and structure them when they babbled. I was going to really have to concentrate on the game now. If I couldn't make our words flesh, I was going to be annihilated. The stakes of the game were looking more and more desperate.

My first mistake was to ask Morgan for help. She told me to take up where I'd left off. She pointed out that I'd already obtruded myself into the relationship between Cell and Sly. She reminded me of my deceptions, of the spiral serpent, of my taking Cell's voice in my blind desire to hear Sly speak to me. She taunted me with the sin she had already made me commit. I resisted. I even argued with her.

—But I don't need to do that any more, Morgan. I don't need to because he's here. He has to speak to me nearly every day anyway. We have a real relationship now, even if he doesn't really like me.

—He never speaks to you the way he speaks to her.

I didn't want to remember the way I'd toyed with Sly before I'd met him. Since Cell nearly drowned everything had changed. We were one body. I wanted to stay a member of our integrated world, giving myself over to our common purpose. I was strict with myself, rationing my exposure to Sly's voice, keeping the spiral serpent tethered.

—Seduce Sly, Morgan suggested. You'll never get a third with those instruments. Not for ages. The only way to get a third fast is to take him. And if you can't do it fast he'll chuck you out anyway. You've got to do it. Do it for Cell.

2 The Needle

I don't know how I did it. I don't know how I was able to do it. I wasn't short of craft—I had as much of that as I had naiveté. So I tried to embroider something of Cell into myself when I was with Sly, some cadence of hers in my voice, some rounded image of her just nudging the sharp edges of me. I could never approximate her plenty but I tried in my own paltry way to suggest it. And it was working. He saw the glimpses of her in me and he came close to look. I think that was what made him come. I don't know otherwise why someone like him would be interested in me.

But he was. He *was* interested in me. Something held him.

Then there were strings. I mean my attraction. I started somehow to pull on him, like I had some control over him. I thought at first that it was just the tension of our three-way conspiracy, the taut interrelationship which we had inhabited for the last months. It was natural, obsessed as we all were with my body, what went on in my mingy insides, that he'd get caught up in the act of looking at me.

But it was more than that. I had begun to intrigue him. My sparseness stopped being ugly. My twiggy body stretched its crooked slender bits and pieces, meshed itself into something else, and started to look sexy.

He didn't notice this growing in him.

Until one month he asked, Well?

And I told him, not yet.

The pause then had a taste of something unsaid in it.

A shudder went through me. A delicious shudder. Around me I felt the ectoplasmic presence of my mother, rich and cloying in her incarnation of the demon Lilith, queen of nightmares and sinful dreams. Sinuous, she stroked my entire pelt and she made my hair stand on end, my legs tremor and heat, my breasts tight. Her twigged fingers enlivened the evil corps of all my suppressed and nauseating thoughts, which chorused loud as the rainforest on a rainy night. I myself caught the scent coming off me, a powerful musky animal whiff that dizzied me as it was released into the primed air under those delectable and dread ministrations. Her caresses were a message, an instruction. They were also a perfectly conceived snare. It was in vain to importune that harsh and wily mistress. She had determined that I was to follow in her footsteps, track that same rustmuddy path into shade and decay, bewitchment and faithlessness, that she had worn into being. Adulterous fiend she prodded me.

This is my refuge. Perhaps it was not me at all who was the agent in what came next, but the beautiful and seductive dream, sheathed in Lilith's spell, which I became. Here in my trance, I became Lilith's demon host. In her witching I could have had anyone. But my argument for my powerlessness in the face of destiny must also hinge on the fact that my preparation for this moment went even beyond Morgan's science, for it was certain that the Warlock had had a hand in it too. Of course the face and body which he had made for me, so enigmatic, beauteous and compelling to those who troubled to look, had the magnetism which went with the very best spells, and it was no doubt in a large part due to this that I was able, under the lethal influence of the demon Lilith's incantations, to qualify as Sly's succubus. For at last he really looked at me, and this was his undoing.

We were standing at the land end of the wharf. I could see the back of the wharf writhing, snake-like, in the moonlight, every boned plank luminous. I knew it was alive with possibilities, a fluid path. Everything was possible, everything was mobile and dynamic and strange. Looking out across the bay I could see a crack in the harbour waters, basted by the full moon, where the dark possibilities were surging forth, stirring the air with their new membranous wings, crowing into the silver sky.

The night air grew so heavy with the something unsaid that Sly finally took both my shoulders in his hands and fell over himself to land in those suction pool eyes of Morgan's. They were all awash, because I was crying. He swam there a while, flipped in me.

That was the moment when he saw my beauty—apprehended it dancing crazy, self-destructive like a moth flickering around a light. He couldn't believe he hadn't noticed it before, since in that moment he was consumed by the perfect angularity of my face, and the two suction pools set deep in it, asking for trouble, and my lips open a little and trembling—with fear? No—with longing. It dawned on him, floating on his back, upended in me, that I longed to please him.

—What is it, Dimity? For the first time, he used my name.

—I'm sorry, Sly. I'm really sorry.

—Why? You don't want to go through with it?

—God no, it's not that. I really . . . I really want to help you. It's just . . .

—Just what? Dimity, you're trembling. Are you all right? Just what?

—Just that I don't know if it will work. Not like that, not with . . . the jars and things. I'm doing it right I promise, Sly, I'm doing it just how I was told but I just don't know if it can happen, without the physical . . . part. I think my body's saying no, Sly. I'm really sorry but I just don't know if my body can start it like this, without without without . . . and that can't happen it would be wrong.

To still the trembling lip, he kissed it.

Then he was leading me. Astray. I'll always maintain that it was him who led, whatever my provocation. He clasped my hand and I trailed after him, let him channel me through the seethe of city, to hand me over the stone wall and speared iron palings which enclosed the locked park, uncomplaining even when my inner thigh scraped one of the spears in a stroke of pain. He was pulling me along the path, pulling me along the winding path like a needle inoutin across the wooden bridges that spanned the brook. Was it nine crossings? He took me deep into the shadow valley, the place where the fallen leaves banked up in the very cleft of the city, and he laid me down there in the quiet fronds of the heavy dark garden. Freckled with the full moon he laid me bare in a nest of silver shavings.

I saw him over me just as I always had. He was vast and celestial. His every pore a poem. His being flat and impenetrable, sprawling in its magnificent wide-angle conquest of space. But now I had my chance to see God closer than ever before, and to go solo as his audience.

I offered myself up, pure and simple. No lures, no foreplay, no tantalising, no trying to find what would please him best. How would I know all that stuff? I only knew the surrender, a willing availability. I knew how to submit just like a doll.

But the talking afterwards. That was different. Now that I had him, that rich voice in the mottled darkness, I wanted words. I wound my pithy limbs up and around him like climbing vine and squeezed the words out of him. Of course that was where my need was. I let my need run rampant.

That made him pity me. I mean, how pitiful and human a need was that? To communicate. Except I didn't say much. Mostly I wanted to listen. That was okay by him—after all he was a professional talker. So he talked. Lying beside me in the leaf litter of our new-forged lie he spread the starry sequences of his speech over me like a quilt. I was new to him.

—I'm not used to seeing my audience like this. Even if only by half-light. I mean, night after night I speak to complete strangers, and when I do talkback, they speak back to me. But they're only voices. Emanations from a collective consciousness which I term my listenership.

He'd realised that in me he had, for the first time, a listener who was not disembodied. My listening had the quality of hunger which moulded all else I did. I listened with a devouring attentiveness. I really did hang on his every word. I listened like the most desperate of his fans did.

—You are my audience made flesh.

I suppose that engaged his imagination. Turned him on. Because in the rustle of undergrowth he was kissing my foot until he noticed something which made him stop.

—What the hell is this?

He pointed to my heel. I craned my stalk of a neck to see his finger, pressed hard on the mark there.

—It's a tattoo.

—What's it for?

I didn't want to answer. So he made me. I cried out when I felt my leg twist inwards from the ankle.

—It's for speaking!

—What—a conversation starter?

—A . . . ? Yes. Yes, that's right.

His grasp loosened. His hand moved to my thigh until he pulled it back suddenly. He examined it.

—This isn't the first time?

—No.

—You're bleeding.

—I got a scrape on the fence.

I looked down. There were my two legs, thin as vines. And there was the stain on them. I could clearly see it. Gagging panic to see those red flowers, blackened in the metallic light of moon, but surely blossoming there. Stitched there like tapestry. To match this new secret.

What did we make? What did we sew up there together in the brindled and sequestered glade of Sly's most hidden desires and of my dread secrets? One more silence. One more gag. One more conspiracy. Another surface to maintain. And beneath it, a whole set of strings, trapezes and ropes to negotiate and manipulate.

Part Six

THE IDEA

1 In the First Month

I told Sly and Cell that I was pregnant.

The next thing I know I'm throwing up. I'm sick as sick as sick. It's the idea that is causing it. The conception. I am making myself sick. But it's all in a good cause. If I can bring this idea to term I will win the game.

Everything is locking into a question of belief. To make it, we three, Cell and Sly and I, have to believe in our own creation. Watch out now, don't rock the boat! Do you see the boat rolling when Cell stretches out her hand and bats it lightly, testing its seaworthiness, assessing whether or not it will take us on our journey's end? She's tapping and slapping and probing, looking for cracks in the hull. I can't tell her *hands off!*—not yet. We have to set out on the glassy ocean, still now in the eye of the storm, gleaming silver under black banked cloud spearing it with the bladed sun. We are alone.

2 IN THE SECOND MONTH

Sitting on the wharf at night, I played shadow puppets with Cell. She was trying to find me. She questioned me. I'd never seen her this insistent. We sat there side by side, shins dangling over the sinuous caress of water at the stumped and splintered legs of the wharf, darkness muffling us in secrecy, our shoulders just touching. Look up and you can see the pinpricked sky, stabbed with stars, upholstered shut (just like you). Behind it surely the mass of secrets, packed in close to the darkness on the other side of the sky. Because the sky is really just a purse, with us inside it.

Had our elemental link suddenly absorbed Sly's leachings, his preoccupations with concrete genealogies, histories, family heritage? All the things which I'd managed to steer Cell away from. What I'd told her about my past was unspecific. Before, she drank up the stories which I recounted but categorised them as fairy-tales, full of passions and terrors, naiveté and evil. She saw them as myths. Now she wanted details. She wanted to know about people from my past life. She wanted to know about my mother.

She pressured me so much that I told her I was a

test-tube baby. The pause grew so large in the pursed sky that it impelled me to keep talking.

—That's why I can really sympathise with you. Why I want to give you a chance with this baby. I wouldn't want you to become like my mother. Obsessed. It ruled her life. It just about sent her mad, even though she won the game. As if she couldn't just be a mother after all that. Nine years of complete domination by one idea—I suppose that's enough to send most people a bit crazy.

I had hair in my eyes—strands sleeked across like a nest. I was hiding in there, quirkily assembling more sticks and leaves into my rough woven outer shell. I didn't want to let her into my camouflage. I felt that she was testing me.

—So where are your parents now?

—Now?

—Yeah. They're still alive aren't they?

—Alive? No. No . . . they're dead.

—O. Sorry . . .

Cell was overwhelmingly honest, so she didn't hold back from asking how they died.

—There was a fire. A huge fire. They had a house in the bush. After I left there was a drought—kind of a weird climatic kink that changed everything. There was rainforest there but it was different after the drought had held for a couple of years—nowhere near as wet as it should have been. So when the bushfires came through everything went up. Con . . . Dad was in the house and he couldn't get out. Part of the roof fell in and pinned him to the bed. Morgan had got out but she couldn't find him outside so she ran in and found him stuck there. She was pulling on his legs, trying to get him free, when the rest of the roof caved in and they were both trapped under a tower of flame.

—Hell! That was brave of your mother to go in after your dad.

—Morgan? She was a sati.

—Eh?

—Once women in India were burnt on their husbands' funeral pyres. They were called satis. That's like Morgan. She threw herself on Con's funeral pyre and went down with him.

Even in the darkness I could see that Cell was disturbed. She was looking at me with dread. Suicide frightened her more than anything else, because it was the negation of everything. Murder made more sense to her because it had purpose.

—Why would your mother do that?

—Because she was crazy and she felt sorry. I suppose because she thought she deserved to die. She was a liar. She had an instinct for finding her own punishment.

—Were you there?

—No. I never went there again after I left.

—Then how do you know this? How can you know if you weren't there?

—I know. I know that the fire started because Morgan had too much anger. It was the violence of her anger which killed my father. She was sorry though.

When she realised what she'd done she self-immolated.

—You mean she lit the fire?

—If anyone lit it she did.

—But you said there were bushfires.

—Yes. There were bushfires. Morgan had the biggest anger that those forests had ever seen.

The way she looked at me told me what she was thinking: if this was the truth, I must be projecting it somehow. Throwing it against a wall which showed its huge crooked shadow, not the petty sticky-fingered reality. She called me on it.

—You're lying, Dimity.

—No, it's true.

—No it isn't. You're a liar.

—How can you say that? I challenged. What do you know about me?

I rolled my sleeves up and down the strips of my arms. It was dark enough to conceal the bruises mottled all along them. My fingers twitched like twigs in sporadic winds. Defiance reared up in Cell, as it sometimes did. Her equanimity fell loose. She looked me in the eye. Her head turning straight towards me in a whip of motion, pausing, now aureoled in faint light trickling from the boat.

—Dimity, I know sweet fuckall about you. That's why I'm asking.

—Yet I'm carrying your child!

And that cut her. It really sliced into her. She started wondering what on earth she did know about me. I who was so intimately tied up in her life. Whose body was the stand-in for her own. Who like a stunt actor, was going to perform a miracle and then let her get the credit.

That was the point where I damaged her trust.

—Do you ever think of the baby as yours?

—It can't be mine. It's yours and Sly's.

—But won't you feel differently when it's born and you have to give it up? Even if we are a family. A funny family. We'll have to tell everyone it's mine.

—I don't see myself as a mother.

—But you already are one.

—Perhaps. It's not the future for me though.

—Then what will you do next, when this is done?

—I suppose I'll start looking for a job. A real job.

She laughed.

—Do you ever think about love?

I showed her an innocent yet devious grin, a quirk in the wrapped night.

—Everyone thinks about love.

It was at that moment that I looked up to see a gigantic bird, beak hooked as a scythe, carving its remorseless path across the squeezing sky. I heard it squawk, a phantasmal and foreboding sound in that malevolent and claustrophic night, striking out and wavering like a poorly tuned violin over the black waters of the harbour. And when I looked away, shuddering and remembering the Warlock, my gaze flicked to the land end of the wharf and I saw there a cloaked figure, skulking silently, kept at bay by the power of my white witch.

I looked again to Cell, and sensed her distrustful still. There was her shadowed face where she'd hung her head to watch her rounded calves and the playful twin mammals of her feet, fidgeting in the penumbra. She pulsed in her own queries and uncertainties, the lambent solution of her life clouded with the poison only I could bring it. I realised something very profound and very dangerous: in contaminating her, I had surely diluted her powers. My prickled nape and goosepimpled limbs told me that the figure which haunted me was the Warlock and that in doing Morgan's bidding I was weakening the forcefield I had found in Cell. With every toxic drop of doubt, my protectress would falter and flounder. When things had gotten so bad that she billowed frightened and stupefied in a sea newly polluted and ruby with her own blood, the Warlock would approach. In his grasp would be the tools of his trade, blades and instruments flashing scintillating lights from the black which surrounded him, as he bent his purposeful megalomaniac's genius to the task of capturing his quarry and his princess, the monster that was me.

3 In the Third Month

Inside the boat at night there is the sway and tender cradle. I lie there in my supine soul and think about Sly and Cell. Sometimes Cell lies with me before she goes to the office. Her body is like my own outer shell. Other times Sly lies there with me and holds me, talking, talking, talking.

—You could lacerate Cell you know. You could tell her that it's more than the drive to reproduce, more than casual sex, more even than an obsession. That I love you. That I've ratified this in words. You know that hurts the most, that word love. But you won't will you? It's not how you look at things.

Sly can see that I am a mess of concealments, but accepts that my reasons for involving myself in this crazy scam are those that I have stated to him and to Cell. He knows that I genuinely want to help them.

—You are my own temptress. And you never even seduced me. If anything, I seduced you. But you have power over me. Yet you worship me, don't you?

—I worship Cell.

—And *I* worship *you*.

I flinched. He catches my head in recoil and laughs.

—You're not easy with that. You drink it up like

any woman would. But it's not real to you, is it? I love you.

My eyes fill with tears.

—These are tears not of sorrow but incredulity, he whispers, wiping them off.

He likes to lie next to me with his head poised on my belly, listening. He says he can hear sounds, and is convinced that they are messages from his child.

—I can hear him.

—Who?

—The baby, silly.

My hands are clasping his head, rasping against his whiskers, as I feebly try to lift him away from there.

—It's too heavy.

—Can you feel the baby in there?

I don't answer. My eyes glide aimlessly around the edges of the half-life.

—Dim, are you listening to me?

—Mmm?

—Can you feel the baby yet?

—No. Not yet.

He starts to kiss my belly. I lie still, receiving it as I always do.

—Dim?

—Mmm?

—Will you tell Cell?

—What?

—About this. That it wasn't the syringes that started the baby. That I went to bed with you.

—No.

—Never? No matter what happens?

—No, never.

—Who do you love the most, me or Cell?

I was serious, considering. And then I laughed, another evasion.

Under my pillow he finds the pearls.

—What's this! Valium tablets?

I don't answer. I just make a grab for them.

—Dim! These are for bored housewives, not pregnant mothers.

—That's a cliché. They help me stay calm. It's weird here, being alone at night. I need help to stay calm.

—Don't be stupid. They can't be good for the baby.

—It's not good for anyone if I'm scared.

He pulls me into the bathroom and makes me watch while he holds the bottle over the toilet. It is humiliating—I actually jump up and try to wrench it from his uplifted hand. He twists me tight around and the tablets fall twirly-whirly and tinkling into the toilet bowl, a little shower of pearls plopping into water and piling up underwater, like a treasure. He presses the button and they churn. Most go down but some stay there, clustered in the cup of the toilet bowl. He leaves them there because he doesn't expect me to fish them out later on, mostly dissolved.

—Next time you're scared call me, okay? You don't need this shit, this'll just make you weak. You've got to be strong. Remember you're living for another person now. Everything you do has to take that person into account.

Sly's scrutiny disturbs and frightens me, because I have been invisible for so long. Can you imagine, Cell and Sly, what it is like to have someone check for liquor, cigarettes, prescription drugs, fastfood packets? To have someone ask you if you've taken your vitamins, done your exercises, been to your doctor/midwife/classes/support group meetings? Police you really. Because that's what Sly is doing. He checks up on me, supervises my diet, asks me about my habits, lectures me when they don't meet specifications.

Always he fans over me like a big budget film. His extensive plane of presence surveying me, the eagling eye for detail niggling. Beneath this landscape my stick figure can only waver in a blur of heat.

Yes, Sly. I did worship Cell. And I did worship you too. I still do.

But Cell cast me off. And you left me there—remember? You left me in the isolation unit she devised for me. Even though you said you loved me.

But the joke is on you. If you look you'll see what Lock left me with, and I'm not talking about the mercurochrome. But no more of that, that's all behind me. No more bleeding because it has been decided that all that will stop. The idea has put a stop to it. The third will make sure that there will be no more blood.

I drink fifteen or twenty glasses of water a day, and I wet myself sometimes. There's no doubt that the idea is changing my body. I bloat and push the perimeter out. I crave certain foods and try to feed the idea on them, but there is a lot of vomiting because it makes me sick. I'm scared to get fat but I must nourish the idea so my body tugs and pulls, binges and purges. I laugh and cry and become violently angry in the space of minutes. I am living on the very edge of my body as it is taken over by this third—the very conception that I begged for and then finally generated myself becomes a usurper, and I its captive.

I cannot predict what the next months will bring. I have five more months where this idea can occupy me, but after that I will have to hand it over. The third will come bawling and tantruming into the world, recognisable now as just another attempt to get attention. Ultimately inauthentic, not mine. Not real—just another sequence in the same nightmare. Something I dreamed and drew Cell and Sly into. A dream which they'll take over when it comes to term and bear off to its conclusion.

In the end I know that they will cast me off. They will knit up their relation, turn their backs and refuse me access to their close sealed new world.

This is my dread. I cup it against me, cradle it, feed it from my own tortures. Over time, it grows as big as the conception itself is growing. They become twins, my idea interlacing with my dread, nourished on the same cord which knots them tightly together, so close they'll surely be strangled?

How did Cell turn? It happened gradually and yet all of a sudden. It was my fault that she finally bit back—I baited her. In my own delirium I didn't think to preserve the solidarity which we'd had. I didn't realise how lost I would feel when she cut me adrift. I toyed with her, not considering the consequences. Dangling off the mother ship, my crude little raft flirty on the giant swells, inconsequential, blind to its unsound structure and the loosening knots which lashed log to log, the fraying cords against which the voices chafed and struggled. I hadn't taken into account the possibility that the line that bound me to her might just break. My success had made me stupid, made me forget that my weakness was my only strength, trapped me in a ridiculous fallacy that I had unqualified power.

But of course I was crazy by then. Well and truly crazy. Swollen with my very own interpretation of the curse, I was in love with Sly's voice and my whole world was becoming narrowed into the short periods he spent alone with me.

I'd lie out under the panorama of his face, receiving him, and then his voice would unfurl out of his superhuman surface and grant me meaning. I clung on there beneath the full-bodied span of his larger-than-life existence, fingers splayed out and thrust against whatever purchase I could find on the smooth surface of Sly's reality. I was bug-eyed and begging for sustenance.

When he wasn't there I licked in seclusion at the pearls and contemplated the washing quiet world of my own lost treasures, better concealed now.

But what of Cell? Of course she would have to find out one day about the adulterous loves of her man and her friend. People that strong don't collapse and die like I would. They fight back, with whatever weapons they can muster. Who can blame her really? Perhaps I would have done the same, if I had been Cell (by this time I almost was). When Cell turned, she lost what remained of her trust and fellow feeling, and surrendered herself to her instinct. From then on we were pitted against one another, and both of us knew it.

I think this was the spot.

That time when Cell came swoopcurve in the liquid arch of another dawn, diving below deck to find me curled up naked on my little bunk in the tiny warm underwater cave of my life. She sees that I sleep like a child. But I'm bigger now. My belly is just a little round. Cell leaps up, careful not to knock precious me as I curl into consciousness, slow and languid and detached as a cat. She is only just clinging to the edge of the narrow bunk, and I deliberately move closer to the panelling so that there will be more room for Cell. As she heaves herself onto the mattress it is inevitable that she will notice that it is wet in the centre.

—Did you spill something?

I burst out laughing.

—Yes.

—What's funny?

—Nothing, Cell, nothing. Only the tide coming in, only the tide foaming at the edges as it comes in, tickling me all over starting at the toes . . . can't you smell the sea coming in?

—No, Dim. No sea.

—O yes, surely the sea? The salty sea which has splashed me and made the bunk wet. The boat has sprung a leak.

I know that she understood. She didn't know the substance of her understanding, but it expanded in her gut like another conception altogether. And suddenly, she wanted me out.

Lying in my bunk and watching I can see the polished

curved back and the ringlets looping down and I lavish yearning looks there. My eyelids flutter in my head in anticipation of the hand of God (which once cupped me like a doll) doing something else altogether. The invisible hand which picks up one contoured part and puts it to invisible lips and an invisible ear, whilst the other hand, unseen, is pressing. And me—not entirely ignorant of all this divine action, I am lying there expectant. I listen for the trilling call into the other world where we are talking. In that world we are nowhere at all. There are two different places (there and here) but we exist as voices exchanging somewhere else altogether. In virtual reality.

I am rolling about in the sheets and giggling because I can't wait. I am so excited. There's the slow heat rising because I am so in love with the voice that I am affected deep. There is no explanation. Only the sovereignty. The chords, striking right in there. Everything quickens. That is mastery.

Sure enough the phone is ringing and I'm speaking to Sly who is telling me something bad. He is telling me that Cell wants me to move out. Telling me without protest, with resignation and fatigue in his voice. He is rationalising it—because it will be better for the three of us not to be living in each other's pockets, it will be more healthy for us to maintain some kind of distance, it wouldn't be right for us to live some kind of triangle relationship because obviously when the baby is born there will be a new triangle surely? Anyway, he's leaving to do another series of talkbacks for the next month. He'll make sure I've got somewhere to go before he catches the plane. He'll make sure I've got suitable surrounds for the coming months.

In fact he has the perfect place in mind. He and Cell have a wonderful rural retreat, the ideal place for a pregnant woman to go and commune with nature. He knows I am going to love it. And I am not to worry, as he will visit me as often as he can. Cell needs some space, but I have her full support in my magnificent task of bringing the baby to term. I am not to worry if Cell is quiet for a little while. It is hard for her having a baby like this. I am assured that Sly will provide me with everything I need. I will want for nothing. Nothing at all.

Watch the plump love go pop and the poor heart go flat before the nails come out and one little scratch before I black out.

—So I'm just the incubator now for you and Cell's bouncing new baby?

Yes, I faint to the floor and it is Morgan who picks me up and slaps me around until I come to. Sly's voice is still bleating from the earpiece of the phone, twirling from the wall on the stretched-out end of its cord. Morgan takes me by the shoulders and gives me a good shake. Then she hangs up on him.

Part Seven

MESSAGES FROM MORGAN

1 Poison Tongue

Ceremony.

Prayer.

Aphrodisiacs.

Medicine.

We tried everything.

I remember us with the lovedust on our skins, creasing into our pores until we were crazed, cracked, mad like clay pots coming to pieces. There were crevices everywhere.

A portent, I think, of what was to come. Our cracked child, our poor broken baby, our curious little doll with not a single orifice in the right place, but holes all over nevertheless.

Not a real baby.

It was Mimi, our spirit child. The lanky temptation of our every frustration and our compulsive dreams.

Not a real baby.

A totem.

A voodoo doll.

The spell which bound us.

The cave spirit which kissed us. Condemned us, and then moved on.

God, I'm raving. Why don't you ring? Please

darling ring me. Can't you tell I'm going crazy? Message after message on this goddamned machine and why the fuck. Why the fuck don't you ever ring me back, you trenchant asshole?

Later that night, when she was in bed, the phone rang again. The answering machine clicked on.

—Hi. You've got Celeste. I'm too scared to come to the phone right now. If you'd like to leave a message, just talk after the beep.

Beep. A man's voice.

Honey I've been waiting for days to hear from you. Just got back from Cairns. Did you get any of my messages? I've left details so often I've lost count. Once more for the record: I'm at Alistair's, over at Coogee. Jesus darling why don't you ring me up some time and we can get together. I promise I'll listen. I've understood most of what you said to me. Sure, it took me a few months but I get it now, I really do. I need to talk to you. About everything. But especially . . . especially . . . about the child. Clay isn't enough. Please, please, please just ring me.

Cell was trembling. How to stop the messages, how to get these people off her phone. Why, when her voice came on, didn't these callers realise that they had the wrong number? They didn't care that she didn't know who they were. They left messages anyway. Messages that weren't even addressed to her. But the baby, the child that they talked about constantly. Not our baby, she kept saying to herself. It's not our baby that they mean. It turned into a question. Her dreams were studded with it. *It's not our baby that they mean? Not our baby? Not that baby that they mean?*

Cell didn't know what she thought about the baby any more. She couldn't see it as real, not now that the whole idea of it had been banished. It had been three weeks. But it was coming back to haunt her. Like babies do. I know. She was only just finding out.

There again, the ringing, her voice coming off the tape. Beep.

—Cell? What's all this shit about you being scared? It's Sly. If you're there, pick up the phone. Cell?

She picked up the phone, breathless.

—Hi.

—What's up with you?

—While you've been gone strangers have been calling me and leaving messages on the answering machine and I'm too scared to pick up the phone.

—You don't know who it is?

—No. At first I thought Dim had something to do with it. I don't trust her. God, I don't know. It's not her voice, Sly. One of the callers is a man. And they're not talking to me, they're talking to each other. But it's strange. It's not like a wrong number. Not so simple. The messages seem directed at us in some way . . .

—What kind of messages? Have you still got them on tape?

—Just the last one.

—Look, I called to say that I'm on schedule. My plane's leaving now. I'll be there as soon as I can. Don't erase the message, will you? And don't pick up the phone. And don't leave, alright?

—Okay. Promise you won't go away like this again until things are normal?

—I promise. Gotta go, the plane's about to take off.

—Hurry up then, I need you. Bye.

Cell played Sly the last message on the answering machine. Since he'd called, there had been another one.

We had a dream.

And it turned into a nightmare.

Common enough, you say, that happens all the time. What's so weird about that?

Nothing then I suppose. Nothing at all.

The dream some nights went like this.

I am lying in bed alone, and the incubus comes to me. The black mantilla frills of its hair and the stiff bristles along its back and neck are outlined in moon, as it puts one sure hand to the coverlet and rolls it back like skin to bare the bone beneath—my body—pliant to its sicklied delicious will. The silver air is shuddering at its acid breath. So am I. I have a mouth wrapped and gagged in dreams and entwined in poison tongue roiling with flattery, deceit, lust, mistrust, boastfulness and all the language of misconception. Noxious fancies crowd at door and windows, the shadowy ministrations of the demon wraith are fear and pleasure and black desire that turns the room clammy.

Of that riding nightmare a child was made. An odd progeny that I called after the darkness.

—Bloody hell. Are they all like this?

—That's the most extreme one yet. I just don't understand. I mean who would ring up to say that kind of stuff? It's two people who ring up. A woman and a man. I'm pretty sure it's the same two people all the time. It's as if they're talking to each other, having a conversation.

—But each one never gets to hear what the other one has to say.

—Yeah. Weird eh? But they're on about the same stuff. All this talk of a child . . . do you think someone knows? Maybe someone's found out. It's not legal really, is it? The setup with Dimity. Perhaps there's some creep out there who wants to blackmail us or something. Do you think that's possible?

He looked blank, shrugged, asked, Did you ring Telecom?

—Didn't think of it.

—We'd better. They can trace the calls. Worth ringing the police too.

—I've been a phone abuser for years.

Sly looked surprised.

—What?

—Yeah. You know, the phone sex. And I had one of those toll numbers before that. I set it up to make some money. I've never paid a phone bill in my life and I stole a mobile phone once. I've got this set of telecommunications misdemeanours. It's like the system has its revenge.

Sly was laughing so loud she could feel it in her chest.

—I'm glad you've still got a sense of humour about this, he murmured.

Cell grinned her juiciest and it was a pulley, because its arch pulled him towards her across that big open room, so close that she teased, Well then Sly honeypie have you got enough in there after three weeks rest enough in there for something special something now here with me . . . ? and the questions were swallowed up in kisses enveloped in a long drawn-out gasp of flesh saying yes giggling into the wheat field, the open swaying sea washing them through and out and over into the other world where they made love and forgot about Morgan, who didn't forget about them.

2 Burst the Cell

In the darkness there was Cell, a blueblack inky radiance of consciousness, pulsing in a patina of her own light, which leaked through the membranous borders of her being. Pressed up against her and webbed with a companion aura, Sly tremored in his own fluid indigo centre. In a streaming luminescent glow, these two nudged, bumped slipperyslidy, and interlocked. A current fused them in space and time. The breathing rolling effulgent (new) form quivered in the heart of the universe, which sucked against it (impartial, amorous, vast, oceanic).

If they thought that becoming one thing would shut out the fragmentation, seal them up in their beautiful world which existed before Morgan and her sprite found them, they were wrong. Morgan had their number. And she wasn't scared to ring their bell. Not only that, but darkness was her habitat and converting it to nightmare her specialty.

Accordingly sound sliced their pod open, split its liquid codings into redifferentiated space. Objects rushed into definition, identity slapped helter-skelter and insistent into the world, and they weren't allowed to be one thing any more. Tumbled apart in a tangle of their separate limbs, sticky and shocked, they scrambled in a panic on their bed, lifting their hunted noses to the low roof of the cabin. If the sound, raw and ringing, was a sword, it only got in two stabs before their answering machine clicked in to silence it with speech.

—Hi. You've got Celeste. I'm too scared to come to the phone right now. If you'd like to leave a message, just talk after the beep.

Beep. Then came the answer.

I know you're there and I can see you. I can see both of you. I know what you are doing. I can see you fucking. Stop now, because if you don't I'm going to hurt you.

3 Kiss the Barb

Well yes I Morgan am watching them. Yes I am watching and waiting and biding my time. Why should they be alone? In any conception there are not two but three progenitors. Otherwise it can't work. I know this because of experience. This being the past it is of course present and future, through the black cloud that is the body of time. That is what the universe is about—curses repeated, births rehashed, conceptions which will not go away but haunt like wilful ghosts.

The demon host is entertained and thus there is the idea of a baby. That's how I see it.

So when two are lying, why should the third not lie with them?

And when two are making but there is nothing made, why should the third not join in?

And when two exploit and manipulate, there is always room for a third who has better skills, whose hands know sleight, whose thirst is never slaked, whose belly is a lean mystery and whose mind is honeycombed and dark as an ants' nest, whose voice is many and whose heart is riven.

Surely we are speaking now of that dishonest sprite, that changeling, my own little child of the dark kingdom? My child lives in strain. She lives out her small inheritance, which is vested in strain. Through strain she has breath; strain and the hand of the third. Through strain she was born into her first life, and through each life thereafter. So here she is, at war now with a woman who is oozy yet one, fighting it out now with one who is her sister yet her enemy, mindgaming it with a pair who have no idea of the viciousness of the stakes but like everyone they are greedy for the third, and they are reeling the third into their lives like misguided children eagerly reel in poison whiskered catfish.

I won't counsel her against biting their bait. There is a hook-shaped tadpole, it is proffered to my snake-tongued child who will give it a lick. One tongue coiling around another, she is trying to lasso that potency for herself. She is kissing the barb, silly child. She has taken the barb so deep now that there is no getting it out again without wounds. She is digesting the end before she is even halfway there!

She has also made the mistake of trying to replace me. Mewling, she calls that lumpen thing mother in her heart. The brat misleads herself. One moment she knows the truth, knows this woman Cell is her sister, the next she tries to deceive herself and call her mother. As if you can have a different mother to the one that you have by ancestry and destiny both, just by wishing. Just as I could never have any other child but this wretched brat I called Dim, she can never replace me as her parent. Her self-delusion is comedy to me. I'm laughing in the smoke of the volcano because I know that woman is not mother but sister, the yang to my baby's yin, the other half of a capsule locked in opposition. I am mother, and no other.

Swallow the capsule hook line and sinker, kiddo. Wolf it down to your ravenous soul and don't ask why there is only more clawing there. We can't help but gouge in this world where there is only fighting.

And when we are sick of the gouging and our time is up there is always the fire. But only when our time is up. We cannot leave until the game is finished.

Part Eight

JUST DESERT

1 In the Barren

I am compelled now to show you the place where I came from last. I barely know it myself, since I have only ever been there in my worst nightmare.

When I am deep in the shadow valley sleep, I look over my shoulder and the sands run straight towards me, almost burying me as I wend my way into the tunnel, which twists through earth like a needle inoutin nine times. Perhaps this is the selfsame needle that stitched up your lips, and embroidered closed your eyelids that wanted to look.

We go deep into the cave, deep into that cleft where all the dire promises bank up like shifting sands. Out the other side is the barren land where Cell and Sly abandoned me and left me to die. They sent me to the desert, to live in a pyramid of their devising. But the needle is still in my hand.

They were consumers, Cell and Sly. They ate life up as though they were honoured guests at a banquet. They savoured life's opposites. Perhaps that was why they had got themselves a holiday house out west, a dwelling hours away from their floating home on the harbour. They must have relished the wonderful contrast between their little wooden retreat and their weekday home. The economical shape of their pyramid rose up from the desert sands, an improbable and bizarre structure. No one else had thought to build anything in that place—the house stood completely alone in the middle of nowhere. It was near a highway which carried not more than one or two cars in a day. Once a week there was a bus. The two ends of the road receded dizzyingly into the shimmer of horizon. It was to this isolated and desolate place that they bundled me, their sick and tranquillised stray, when things got too hot for them.

Sly came back to the boat after Cell had delivered her ultimatum. He was worried because Morgan had hung up on him. He found me stupefied with valium, alcohol and a visceral despair. If you can manage a laugh now to see the tables turned, savour it while you can. For Sly took the precaution of tying my wrists and ankles, blindfolding me and gagging my mouth before he carried me off the deck of the boat in an easy leap and hurried down the wharf to load me into his prestige car, careful not to bump or shock my stomach. I didn't resist. What would have been the point? My ejection from that safe place was inevitable and my separation from my protectress assured. It was all going to plan. In the fug of my addled mind I heard Morgan laughing, long and low and consistent, as if she was satisfied.

Even in the haze of drugs I was conscious of some small good fortune—the kidnappers were independent agents and were not in the service of the Warlock. I haven't told you, but I did see his shadow more than once, waiting with clear impatience at the end of the wharf. He hovered at the periphery of my life as a buzzard hovers over carrion, waiting for Morgan to yield me up to him. Stupid stupid me, covering my eyes when I sighted him, keeping his sentinel presence wrapped up and hid away with the rest of my secrets, labouring under yet another delusion that if I deceived myself I could outwit my destiny! I didn't tell *you* how often I saw him because I know you would hate me for being stupid and perverse enough to harpoon my white witch. You can't help but accuse: why did I work to wound Cell, the one person who could love me enough to keep me safe, knowing that when she threw me out the Warlock himself was ready and waiting to salvage the scraps? I know it is hard for you to like me when I act so badly, so self-destructively. How can you love someone so enslaved to wickedness as I?

When I woke up the next day then, I walked to the window, and while I stared in shellshocked disbelief at the dead world outside, I was very slightly comforted by the fact that here was a place so freakishly remote that the Warlock would never, in all his born days and with the aid of all his phalanx of familiars, track me down. Such puny comforts are all such creatures as I can hope to receive. Numb, I explored the pyramid. It was tiny, minimalist. One room containing simply a wrought iron double bed, two inhospitable metal chairs, a crude table and a basic kitchen. But in a hatch in the floor there was a giant freezer full of food that looked as if it would last me for months and a note, instructing me to make myself at home and call if I needed anything. By the time I read it, Sly noted cheerily, he would be on the plane. He didn't include the phone number at his new destination.

After the shock of my banishment, I went walking in the sands around my pyramid house. There was complete silence. A silence so bare and so resonant of nothing that I remembered the cicadas. It was as if this silence was so intense that it answered them.

There were no trees. Only the endless flat of the stubbled ground, rumpled with the cold evening winds, broken by outbreaks of blistered boulders interspersed with stunted bushes. By day, there was a baking heat and stillness. A frightening vacancy, possessed by amazing colours. In the mornings and evenings especially, the violets, ultramarines, oranges and pinks would surge.

But even if this was the emptiest place I'd ever been, someone else lived here. And do you know who that someone was? My tongue, that's who. I can prove it.

When you look over there you will see a small hole. The soil is red, and the hole appears a deep magenta in its own shade. Inside there lives my tongue. I know this because I came tripping through here yesterday and discovered the spiral serpent stretched out, basking in the tireless sun. The spiral serpent was scaled red and ochre and white. It knew me straight away, but it did not show it. It moved quickly. Shot through the hole. As if to say, you're not ready for me yet.

But it wasn't long before I was ready. It wasn't long before I was able to pick up the phone and start calling

Cell, knowing that she was alone, knowing that I could really scare her. There was far too much that she didn't know about me. That made it very easy to scare her. After all, I'd never even told her that I was gifted. And of course I had Morgan's full support.

Remember the lyrebird in the forest? Deep in the interlocking bush, scratching into hiding via drifts of leaf litter, the lyrebird reproduces all the other bird sounds. So when you are standing outside its lair, you can hear the transmission of a whole forest full of birds. But really there is one bird only, nestling into its sham. But the bird isn't a mimic because it is deceitful, treacherous or scheming. It is a mimic because that is its nature. And for every trickery it practises, there is a wildcat cloaked in bird feathers, creeping closer, creeping consciously towards its vocal prey. Who is the traitor—the liar bird or the feral cat which will have its life?

If it is true that I was stalking, it is just as true that I was being stalked.

Morgan. Well she'd cursed me. But in the fire, the fire where she and Con perished with all their memorabilia, documentation, everything—in the fire I saw her grinning the second part of the curse. As the black had the edges of her she howled from the pit of the pain, and her mouth bowed out tight to a curve of lost horizons. And from that place came screaming the demon birds of hell, hordes of them shadows in the flames, the jagged shadows carrying the curse out of the volcano and winging their way direct to me to drop it down on me, safe delivered. And Morgan, perished surely? But the curse . . . Was there ever a time when Morgan didn't get what she wanted? Morgan's wishes, however improbable, always came true. I was testimony to that fact of her potency. From the barren land came Morgan's curse—that I would inherit her death. Worse still, her life.

2 Buried Alive

I knew Morgan was winning the day I saw the red flowers. I had been walking every day, skimming through the desert like a spider, hush and I was gone. I glazed the sands with tiny tread, I glided over pebbles and trailed around boulders, I sifted through the bushes. Intent, busy, I dangled in space sometimes to pause and plan. I threaded my path in superstitious intricacy.

That was because on one of the early days that I had ventured out, I had been channelled into the secret cul-de-sac at the far edge of the horizon and discovered the thorn bushes. These were the biggest thorn bushes I had ever seen. They were higher than me, banked up against an escarpment of orange rock about two metres high. The escarpment curved around and created an enclosure which could only be reached by a narrow passage between two tumbled rows of boulders. Once I'd discovered this place, I avoided it. I laced around it, back and forth, back and forth. I networked the terrain rather than confronting taboo at its centre.

The day I saw the flowers I had been scuffling through the sands, peering at the ground for signs. There were a lot of signs. The arcing tracery of the spiral serpent was visible everywhere. There were also bird footprints, and tiny animal dung. Lizards skittered at my creeping tread. Acrid miniature plants mingled austerely with rusted gold pebbles.

I was following my own elaborate rules until I saw the spiral serpent. I was so excited to see the flick and coil of it that I gave chase. Before I knew it I'd arrived at the cul-de-sac of the thorn bushes.

The spiral serpent had vanished in the centre of the stand of thorns.

I was not prepared to see them, clustered on the thorn bushes. Against the purple barbs the flowers were virulently red. They were new—the first time I had found the thorn bushes there were no flowers. I walked up close to them, my breath tangling barbed wire in my lungs. And just as I reached out my hand and touched the flared crimson centre of a blossom, a long black shadow came from behind me, stretching out and past me. It was as if that black shadow had struck me down. Falling, I brushed the thorns and drew blood.

Lying on the ground I looked around. Blocking the passage was the upright figure of the Warlock. I don't know how he found me in that remote and hostile place. Morgan would have tipped him off.

Even though he must have been following me, he still looked surprised. Perhaps because I had changed. The idea had changed me. I was not the same ghost anymore. I was a different ghost altogether.

I jumped up and tried to scale the escarpment to the side of the thorn bushes.

—Stop!

He made me. He'd run after me and seized my ankles, yanking me back to a puff of sand. He had a hold of my neck. He was crushing my delicate spider limbs, my dragonfly wings, my feathered edges where they resisted his insistence. The dust bloomed thick in air.

I was crying, pleading with Morgan.

—Please Morgan let me go now, don't make me, please don't let the Warlock have me!

—Cut the shit. Go on, shut up right now or I'll make you.

His hands around my neck made the threat a promise.

He told me he couldn't believe his luck. He told me he missed me. He told me he was going to have me and if I said no he would make me.

—But you have already made me, Warlock.

—Not that again. Shut up and listen to me.

He told me he'd nearly gone crazy after I left. I wasn't like the others. They were disposable. Just toys. But I was special. I was the connoisseur's cream, the collector's item which could never be parted with, never traded or sold. Sure, it could be polished and restored and its imperfections could even be corrected so that the original design would be as faithfully reproduced as possible. But he would never let me leave again, and he was going to marry me.

He made me take him to the pyramid. He came inside and looked around. Then the hands were on me again and I saw what I had not seen for a good while. I mean the red flowers. The same ones I had been avoiding out there in the desert. The red flowers tumbling out of a blank sky, which neither received or denied my crying, just drowned it in a storm of its own devising.

—Please not the flowers.

—Dim, cut the crap, okay? We both know that this stuff you talk about, flowers and warlock and bloody Barbarella are complete nonsense. Who the hell is Morgan anyway?

—My mother. Morgan is my mother.

—Nonsense. We both know your mother's name is . . .

—No! Morgan is my mother, Morgan is my mother, Morgan is my mother . . .

On and on and on, the repetition. It maddened the Warlock. He loomed over me and shouted to the desiccated sky. Behind him wind cracked. He'd made the sky open up again, just like before. He was powerful. He was casting spells, Morgan's familiar, me *his* familiar. The black cat, fur matted, cowered against the crook of wall and wardrobe. She dared not mew because there was anger scathing her. The Warlock picked her up by the scruff of her neck and dangled her in air. She was always having to live this moment again—a terrible attenuated moment where there was suspension followed by certain violence.

The Warlock tried not to. The effort was visible in his face. It twisted black in the flash of electricity zipping up the outside world in the bodybag tailor-made for it. Outside, there was a dreadful howl of the windstorm which the Warlock had conjured up out of his anger.

He clinched it by asking his familiar, Do you love me?

And the familiar, wretched, daubed in her own sweaty pelt, was for once honest even though the fear dwarfed her, and she looked him in his eyes, crying little mewling tired gasps, and told him, No.

—Is there someone else?

How could the familiar say what she said? She was stronger than anyone thought, even herself. She was so strong she told the truth twice in one night. She told the Warlock, Yes, There are two, master. And if you count it another way, there are three.

He hit me. He had me up against the wardrobe and he was smacking me with the flat of his hand. He didn't want to hit my face. Not his signature. Only a fool would deface his own mark. He concentrated elsewhere. At first he restrained himself, trying not to bruise me. But there were the flowers. He kneed me in the stomach, and just as he did so there was a rasping in the lock and Sly, stupefied, was standing in the oblong frame of the door, his key extended in one hand, his big mouth open in shock as the Warlock let go his hold and I slid, doubled over, to the floor, and lay there completely still. There was a last sporadic flash of hot whistling air before anyone could speak. Then we were in the eye of the whirly-whirly and the whole desert stalled on our outcome.

—What is going on? Sly bawled.

The Warlock glared at him and stood silently over me. I started crying. There was blood on my smock and my insides felt like they were being scraped out from the Warlock kneeing me. The room was undulating in waves of pain and shock.

As the sobs thickened and swelled, Sly ran across the room and crouched down, crying, Dim are you okay? He put out a hand, gingerly spanning my stomach.

—Are you okay here? Dim, is the baby okay?

—Baby! Lock exploded. What the bloody hell . . . ?

He left the door gaping behind him as he left. Resurgent, the dust storm squealed and chafed and red dust began swirling into the room. Coughing, Sly shut the door.

—The flowers. The flowers strewing . . .

—Ssh, it's okay. I'm here now. It's okay.

Sly ran a warm bath and washed me clean. The water was red tinted with blood and dust. I watched the flowers rise up in the bath and bloom in the water, spreading loose until they dissolved. I should have told Sly that there was no point in sponging them free, as they would always be there. They always had been there. These flowers were stains. But I knew he was terrified of what the blood might mean. I had to reassure him. I needed him to believe in me and my conception. We couldn't afford to lose him.

I had to distract him.

—It's so good to see you, Sly. I was beginning to

wonder if I'd ever see you again, ever hear you again.

—I've been away. I couldn't take it. I got myself sent away again.

—I know. You weren't on air.

He took my face and kissed my mouth. He longed, it was clear. But he resisted, because he'd convinced himself that he had to. I was only glad that he still wanted me. I didn't care about anything but that. I lay back in the towel in his arms and I could feel myself sparkling with new happiness. I basked in the heat of his voice, neatly basting the room into something friendly again. I forgot the raging dirt outside.

—Look, I came around here to ask you about the voices.

—The voices . . .

—Yes, there are these voices which . . .

—O yes, I know the voices. I hear them too. I hear them too.

—Don't be funny. On the answering machine, Dim. People have been calling Cell while I've been away and leaving these weird messages on the machine. I know you too well to think you'd do something like that. But someone's doing it and it seems to be related to the arrangement.

—How?

—They're on about a baby. It can't be coincidence. But that's not really important. Not after all this. Who the hell was that guy?

—I knew him before. He found me.

—Did you tell him about us?

—Yes.

—Right.

He was silent for a moment. There were beautiful creases in his cantilevering forehead. I wished he would speak again. My wish came true when he asked, Can you help me about these voices?

I had the perfect solution. It came out like a pearl, all whorled pure and coated with innocence, just like the truth.

—It was him. He did it.

—Who? That guy?

—Yes.

—Why?

—He's a magician. A ventriloquist too. He works in the theatre. He loved me once and he found me. When he found out about the baby he was jealous. He wants me to marry him. He's still in love with me. But he's so jealous. He wanted to pay you back. He wants to hurt you because I'm carrying your baby. He's crazy, Sly.

Sly was furious. He leapt up. He ran to the door. But when he opened it a terrible thing happened. An avalanche of sand came pouring down with a deafening susurration of granule against granule. The sand came and came, more and more of it filling the tiny triangular room of the pyramid, heaping around our helpless ankles and then our knees. We held hands, certain that we were going to die. Right then I'd forgotten all about Madame Futura, all about my nine lives and the promise of my final death. All I could see was the rushing asphyxiating certainties of sand, the running slide of our burial alive.

Of course it was the legacy of the Warlock's frightful anger, the whirling dust storm which he had created as he beat me and which had thickened after him as he left. He'd let it rage, no doubt to punish me.

The sands rose to our mouths. We were gagged by the Warlock's dry fury. Lips clenched close, we waited until they were submerged. Our eyes flickered back and forth. Paralysed, we looked at each other. I would have given anything just to hear Sly's voice one more time before I died. Tears formed on my lashes and ran into the sand, smudging into mud.

Just before our nostrils were stopped up, the avalanche ceased. We had been spared. Sly shifted through the sands, and worked himself loose. He kissed my muddied mouth, cracked in a doll mask smothered in orange dust, and left me there buried in the sand. His voice trailed over the muffling dry stillness.

—Wriggle out. It's easy. I've got to go. Cell doesn't know I'm here.

Sly was in such a hurry to leave and begin the long drive that would get him back to Cell before she found out he was gone, that he didn't even think to tell me what he planned to do about the Warlock.

I stood for a long time, buried in the sediment of disaster. My thoughts were varied and despairing. I asked myself, did anyone know who I was? In all this was there anyone, other than Morgan (now long dead but still a haunting) who could quantify any part of me?

It was as if I was a vast cavern of echoes, eddying

lost, sealed up and silting through dead air like the fallen leaves in the cleft of the valley where I was conceived. Somehow I never got out of that valley, never managed to free myself from the tomb where I was born. Anyone who cooeed into the reverberating sarcophagus simply added to the sediment of voices smothering, compacting, chafing one another. Look! Here comes another bandage spiralling down from the living world, coiling into the silence, layering itself onto the supine forms of me and my mummified mother.

I decided that for me, being born was tantamount to being buried alive. I was solitary. The only person who had ever genuinely been my friend was Cell, a woman who herself had never been alone, not truly, because her warm centre had always drawn companionship from whatever environment she inhabited. It had never been necessary to her to suffer like I had. Her suffering was kicking in now though. Despite her purity it seemed that life had it in for her. I was sorry—I had wanted her perfect equilibrium maintained. She inspired me so much. I was disappointed to see that even she could be touched by the bad dream.

I cried about Cell. Morgan laughed to note that I still had this absurd idea that Cell was the real body of a mother. I felt my painful separation from Cell.

The tears trained through the sand and created a pool around my chin. My head floated there as if I had been decapitated. The moisture roused me from my despair. Squirming my resilient limbs, I loosed the sand and climbed out of my pretend grave.

I unearthed the buried phone, and for some time I waited to find Sly's voice shining out from it. The world could not be dark, could not be light. It was stuck somewhere in between.

Morgan watched me gather myself in the half-light, possessed by the conception and waiting, and her growing madness. She saw me clinging like a stick figure to the window, standing on a peak of sand, watching for predators sometimes, dreaming others.

Nothing happened for what must have been a very long time. Or perhaps only a few hours. Who can say?

The fear and the anger were modulated by boredom. Someone had to act. What else was there for me to do but to take matters into my own hands? What else could I do but deploy my faulty talents?

When Sly, doing his usual nightshift, heard Cell on the other end of the phone, telling him to go and see Dim, he was surprised. He had decided that Cell was now living in a world threatened by jealousy, uncertainty, violence and change, and that she couldn't understand how her joy had given way to this. Understandably, she was trying to make sense of it. So it was an abrupt turnaround. But he understood Cell's compassion; poor Dim had been alone in that house for too long, and she was probably stir crazy. Especially being pregnant.

So he went to visit. When he saw me he could only cry, first because I was so nervous, second because he had missed me so much that seeing me again was like having new eyes. It was like having a whole new body, he thought through the chaos of tears as the polished cool surface of my skin moved slick against his and he slid over and through it to the never never stretching out in the shimmering distance, pebbled with pleasures shining hard, untrustworthy, in the dissolution of the mirage, and always my fluid body ruddering in its angular mysteries, always just ahead, teasing and disappearing, dancing and flying and hopping from foot to foot on the radiant ground. Thrown in light at the end point he understood for the first time the meaning of the phrase, till death do us part.

When he got home and Cell asked him where he had been, and he told her, with Dim, he was amazed at the way her whole face fractured and gave way to madness.

—But you told me to go and visit her.

—What?

—You told me. Remember, you called me today and told me to go there. You said you were worried about her, that you didn't want to make things harder on her. You didn't think it was fair to treat her like she was in solitary confinement. I agreed with you. I mean she is the mother of our child. We can't chuck her out just because we aren't dealing with the situation. She sure as hell doesn't want to be left with the baby.

Cell gaped. Finally she said, Sly, I didn't call you today.

—Yes you did. How can you have forgotten? I'm beginning to worry that you're schizophrenic. We have conversations and then you deny we ever had them.

—Well isn't that strange! And we've got strangers on our phone, an interloper in our lives, a baby that we're calling ours but which never came from us fucking. I mean there are lies just flocking out of the woodwork here! Everywhere I turn there's some kind of lie coming at me. I can't . . .

—Calm down. You're sounding paranoid. For Chrissakes just relax. You're acting like you think the world's out to get you.

Cell was quiet again. The ravelled face meshed back together. But behind it her thoughts were racing wildly towards an uncertain conclusion.

She was going to find her sister.

I told you before that throwing Cell's voice is risky. I did it once before because I have committed myself to verisimilitude. Now that the game has accelerated to the point of decadence, the dangers are so much higher. This sister of mine is resurgent, alive. She can't be contained. As you will see, the power of the huge and torrential ocean is her domain, and she can summon this force to serve her. Now that she is angry, she is a force of nature. Now that she is almost mad, she is at last so like me that she can see through me, anticipate me, and even foil me. In some manner, she *is* me. I have not come this far with my story to watch her debunk it. So I can't help but hesitate when I contemplate the need to impersonate Cell to really show you this part of the story. But don't doubt me. I assure you I am equal to any challenge. Such is the imperious power of my fabulous vocal chords that I have treated you, effortlessly, to a wonderful if dissonant opera of voices past. Cell's voice, though prominent, is just one of a cacophony. So though I don't know now if I should take this risk, I *could* draw myself up and roll out the spiral serpent yet again for your benefit. Know that I am the ventriloquist, and this is my artform.

I hear you trying to influence my decision. Of course, you straitjacketed thing, you want me yet again to prove my power (perhaps you want your revenge, and wish to see me try and fail?). I rise to any challenge. So it is agreed. I have succumbed to your muffled squeakings, themselves a kind of temptation, and let you urge me. A very small concession, made because I have so punished you with this tale. I too, can be kind, for kindness is not just the province of white witches, but of wretches like me. Now, since you want me to prove it can be done, I will throw you the voice of Cell. Listen while I curl my tongue around this new scene, which is like a sequence from an underwater world. You have elected for Cell's truth. Let it be Cell's little tale, her little subaqueous section of the whole. Dive deep now and you will hear of a very great miracle. The miracle of how, after the blinding dust storms that heaped the desert upon itself and buried me, the ocean came to the desert.

3 Cell Invasion

Outside it was oceanic. The tempest surged against the ordinary world and obliterated it. Dusk was coming, but the predusk light was unnaturally forceful, illuminating the totality of the storm, as if from its centre. The new world was a radiant unfamiliar place, slashed with liquid, gushing across sudden sporadic gales and resonating to thunder. Lightning strobed through it but the air was so incandescent it barely registered the influx of more light.

I took this world with me into the plain where Dimity was living. I laboured with the lashing sea to her dwelling. I waited there.

She came out, her face filled with wonder at the turquoise oceans as they washed across the orange expanse of the plain, borne by the current of the storm. In a slate-coloured dress she bowed against the winds, a white umbrella belled over her. I couldn't see her face but I recognised her arms and legs, which were so narrow they seemed only mere slashes, running parallel to the insistent direction of the deluge. With the umbrella over them, her limbs streamed out, edged in light like the tentacles of a box jellyfish. She was so drifting, so delicate and transparent and apparently passive, haunting the currents, making no decisions. Yet this horrible hidden poison!

I had to apprehend her; I knew she was the culprit. The source of all the pain and falseness. But I was anxious then that her nebulous diaphanous form would evade me. How in this shifting world to seize her, voyager in her element of half-truth and outright lie, dangerous toxic slippery creature which would jelly at my touch?

She bobbed before the gate and the umbrella lifted as she scanned my feet-knees-hips-torso-neck-face. In the teeming dissolution of the known she could affect no greeting, no welcome, no falseness. She registered her native vacuity only—a face empty of surprise, or even recognition. Afterwards I had an overwhelming impression of her wide detailed eyes like two starfish set in the belting surf of the rest of her. They were the only uneffaced part. They terrified me in their clarity.

—You have poisoned my life.

She stared. Pinioned by the starfish I seethed in the private other storm of my anger. I grabbed her wasted wrist and wrenched the umbrella loose. I tossed it into the tempest and it was sucked away on the tide. I let go of her, and in the moments which leaked away then she became as wet as I.

—You have poisoned my life, I repeated.

—Cell, this won't be good for the baby.

—Stop hiding behind the baby. Just pretend it doesn't exist, that we only imagined it. You, me and Sly. A stupid game we've been playing.

I couldn't help it. I was so angry I pushed her. She staggered back and her fingers flared desperately in the watery air as she fell. She dropped her hands, which she had been holding close to her body, and lay for a moment in the rushing orange of the ground before she struggled back upright, the starfish so prickly they impaled me.

—You stupid bitch. You fat *whale*. Get out of my way before I claw you up.

I could tell she meant it. I stood back, to see the real her. Only so briefly before she bent and clutched at herself, holding her own body like a shield. The slate-coloured shift, plastered to her nubbed chest and rib cage, slick to her abdomen. And do you know what?

Yes Cell. We do know what. I was five months pregnant and you upended me in the gutter in a howling storm. Then you left, because you realised you were hurting me. You realised that you were running the risk of losing the baby. And that was all you cared about by then, wasn't it Cell?

She lied to Sly about the fight. She told him I'd hit her first. The way she told it sounded like mud wrestling. Two women, their nipples forcing their sopping clothes, wobbling in a watery combat.

Shut up, Cell. Don't try to commandeer my story again. I am the ventriloquist, and I am telling the tale after my own fashion. I will mould your bits for you. You are privileged to be given the voice I have allowed you. You must not overstep the mark.

What she didn't tell Sly was that she was trying to kill me. Or kill the baby. Both.

She dived on top of me, grabbed me by the hair and held me close, the pair of us knotted in the operatic howl of storm and ocean, tossing on the eddying ground. While the waves wrenched our desperate heads, she tried to drown me and failed. But she must have known. She must have known the death that was left. Everything so bloody wet that fire was out of the question, but she my sister, able to intuit the necessary weapon.

She dragged me in a squealing wake to the edge of the pyramid, bracing me there. I had poisoned her life, so she said. So she poisoned mine, leaving me only the two left. Was it she who forced those new pearls down my ripple throat? Backed up against the rising ochre side of the pyramid I swallowed and swallowed and swallowed.

And then she left, gathering her mobile oceanic body and rising up through the sharding red and gold and purple rays of the clearing. She rode the receding storm. I lay there in the lapping orange waters, wrecked and severed. The illusion of the mothership shattered into irrecoverable debris, myself perhaps not salvageable either because for the first time ever since I met Cell, I knew I really was not part of her world. It was all a delusion. I saw myself detached from her. I was separate and lost. Moreover I was dying.

Morgan carried me inside and summoned Sly. She watched over his coming. It was her that realised what was really happening. Astute as ever, she saw that my trinity was coming apart at the seams, that the voice and the body were to be revealed for the petty and useless tinpot amulets that they really were, just one more stupid bargain at the snake oil stall, another futile attempt to fend off the more powerful witchings which are the scourge of life and, she would insist, its point. As she regarded Sly's asinine face, tearsmeared and uncertain, toppled from its bland conviction of control, she saw the significant development, obscured to my own rolling and opalescent eye by the dramatics of dying.

Morgan savoured not only my death by poison, but this more subtle transition which was taking place at one and the same time. Here, she remarked knowingly, was the place that this seventh life unravelled and the eighth one took up the thread, and wasn't it interesting to realise that no matter how battered and divided her daughter had become, she was at least to begin a new life free of the delusion of those idiotic lucky charms? They were only a distraction in the business of enacting destiny. At least, so Morgan thought, relishing her control as she watched the power of Sly's voice falter before her very eyes.

It is true that Morgan's voice was loudest then, so it is fitting that she should preside over this death, as she presided over so many others. Recovered now, my powers fully fledged once more, it is an easy matter to cast her noxious tones into your trapped ear. Morgan tells it.

5 SEVENTH DEATH

Can I show you my child again? For now she is truly a child. Asleep there, numb. This was the greedy child who swallowed all the pearls but never got wisdom. Watch her dive deep in the sea, looking into the goggled face of death. For the seventh time in her short life she lies in the arms of the diver and is wasting there, a corroding treasure never to see more than the weird aqueous half-light which holds her down.

I saw her greet this guest more than once in her childhood. I see her greet it again now. But there is always the interference. The interference is so hard to dispel.

Someone has the pump out. They pump all the half-light away and expose my baby to the bleached world again. Like driftwood she is pallid grey and her limbs are gnarled. She has been tortured. Now she dries out. When she is sentient, she does lament her losses seven.

Listen to Dim as she lolls in her own nausea and curses Cell. Her face is a squashed heart, plastered white. She has hair like spines. Sly's huge head hangs healthy from heaven and his vast voice swaddles her up, sickly child, and makes her promises.

—Fuck you, Cell, you poisoned me. Cell, you poison . . .

—No Dim, not poison, not Cell.

—Deep in the sea lies little drowning, drownded me . . .

—No, you're saved. Listen now Dim, you're saved.

—She is saved only to die again and again.

That man cries. His voice draping down in all its purity suddenly is tearing, a huge rip shreds it from the bottom up, it is unravelling from just the place that my runtling baby has hold of it. Right up into heaven goes the quake, cracking everything open as it goes. Clouds break loose and the light is jostled away until there's only the glowering. Did she see him in shredded garb, power fled?

Part Nine

PENULTIMATE

1 Stillborn

There is no anger like this anger. It is the kind of anger that can only breed violence.

She is counterfeit. Her body is counterfeit. She never once spoke the truth.

If you are listening Dimity, know that I am onto you. I know about each and every one of your lies, I know you probably hate yourself as much as I have to hate you. Attempt your own life? Why not, when you are that hollow? I dare you. I dare you to bring those lies to term. I'll be watching when they urge against the light, cresting a world where they are at last realised, already dead.

Admit, you wretched wretched woman, admit

That was Cell again, trying to break in. You see how she is going crazy, sounding more and more like me. Now more than ever we are like two sides of the same coin, the same voice issuing out of disparate mouths. Both the pawns of the greatest ventriloquist of all, Morgan, we spout her script to a numb and inert audience. Cell though wants to flout the rules. The blubbering cow wants to take over and run the show like she's used to doing. She doesn't like my newfound authority, rebels against my demonstrated independence from her. She doesn't like the fact that our progenitrix, despite her hatred for me, favours me over my adopted sister. Cell at last reveals her pettiness in a display of jealousy over the creature I am becoming, so different to the wraith that she once saved. She writhes and fidgets under my thumb (just like you did when I first lured you into my world!) and will not brook my haloed virtuoso performance as the lyrebird, the beautiful and talented if unlikely star of the story. The ugly duckling made good. You yourself must have marvelled, even sensing the prick of envy, as you have exprienced the power of the drab little brown bird with the magic vocal chords that are bigger than everyone, that can fashion forth the entire world!

But we were talking about Cell. Like any sister she is covetous, competitive. She wants to dominate this my tale and have her say. Not only that, but falsely, villainously, she yearns to denounce me, riddle my yarn with doubt and query. Do you see how she tries to force her way in?

But I've made the rules here, and I have to discipline her. After all, isn't this tale the product of my eight tragically lived lives and their culmination? Isn't this tale the place where I get to have *my* say? For if ever a poor voice was gagged it was mine, if ever a person oppressed it was me. I'm not really feeling sorry for myself. I just reserve the right to keep control of this one area where I have ever had it—this story. You my thrall, quiet and perhaps wearied by me, must hear me out. If Cell is to speak the least she can do is take her turn. It must surely irk you, the presence that will judge, to note that I've only just come back from death but still I have to fend off her shrewings. I have to keep her at bay. The voices, getting out of hand again.

Too many voices! You, Cell, are one too many. What's more you are mad. And I don't just mean angry. Morgan has addled you. And so have I. Your lover has been sleeping with another woman and now he is in love with her, because she has conceived for him. Not only that, but you are very nearly a murderer. Do you see? You have many good reasons to start considering yourself a lunatic.

As I keep trying to explain, the game is in my control. At the helm of the spiral serpent I will account for everything. The truth! What is that? The only truth I can tell you about my body is the one that I have inscribed on my heel. That tattoo is true, inalterable and permanent. The rest is counterfeit, as you would have it. The Warlock made this body for his familiar to live in. I served his conception, and became his monster. Now I make this body the dwelling place of another conception altogether—let's call it our baby. Have we made only another monster?

I know that you're the life force and you will flux in and out of my control. But here, only I can give you presence. My voice, even more powerful it turns out than Sly's (long gone now) is the one which forges this history. So give in. Believe me. That's all there is left for you.

The voices are very hard to manage. There are still the cracks where they argue. Can you see these many cracks? You more than anyone perhaps can see them.

Look at me. I am the clay doll. I lie terracotta in sun and rain and naturally I decompose. My shoulders and thighs are melting, and my features are indistinct.

That's if I make it to old age. The other cycle is quite different. Look again, and you will see the clay doll crazing with the pressures of contradiction, you will see the little fractures creeping and spanning each limb, making a jigsaw of my crude face, until there is so much counterpoint that I simply explode. Powder will return to earth.

Is anyone counting? There are two more left. Only two more. I look the kiln in the face again.

When Madame Futura, passing through the desert on her way to join a new circus on the other side of Australia, saw me dancing there with the bony one dimensionality of my own shadow flickering indigo on the sunset saturated ground, she did not attempt to stop.

In the moments that she had me within her view, squared in the coach window, she noticed that I looked different. The fire had changed me. I had been rebuilt. I was more beautiful than before but unmistakeably myself. It was clear to her that the madness had found me. Just as she had known it would. From her seat in the coach, she could see my two eyes like the big keyholes to a dreadful place. There was scarring inside there. But still the innocence. The innocence that made you forgive because I knew not what I did. I was only following the script.

The coach didn't stop. Even though her destiny was not cuffed to mine, like that of others, Madame Futura still did not beg the driver to let her stop. But she called out, through the crack of window

—You didn't heed my warning about the dissembling!

The dust cloud swallowed the back of the bus. The world blurred chokingly orange. I was glad of only one thing—Madame Futura had survived that first fire through prescience. When it broke out and devoured the freak show, she must have been already gone. It was comforting to know that at least one person had survived the holocaust which surrounded me. Seeing her in those transient moments reminded me that there was more fire left. Plenty more fire left.

What was she thinking as she powered through the night in a spurt of fumes and purposefulness? Probably that I had wanted to tell the truth, but that I did it the wrong way. It never works to save it up until just before the end. If she'd been able to stop the coach that's what she would have told me. So really, she would have reflected as she nestled her feet into her slippers, settled her bracelets on her arm and regarded the unfurling orange plain through the window, what would be the point? Simply to say I told you so? The ending, in any case, remains unchanged, whatever the variables.

3 The Truth

I want to tell the truth. So I tell her. I ring her up. I don't let her say anything.

—I know this is real because I have been really sleeping with Sly. No syringes. I gave that up a long time ago. I've been getting the real thing. And I want to tell you that I am never going to give you your baby. I'm keeping it. It was my idea and I'm keeping it for myself. And just so you'll never take it over, or try to be the winner, I'm going to leave. And do you think that Sly will stay here with you, Cell? He wants his baby more than he wants me or you. And even if in the end maybe he doesn't get it, I will already have won. He told me he loves me. More than once.

Her voice grates because she is so enraged.

—There is no baby. I knew a while ago that you were sleeping with him. You made sure I knew. I don't give a fuck what you do. Just get lost. Sly will find out soon enough.

—Shut up now. He's on his way here right now. He's coming to me because he's scared of you, pacing the house, crying with your tantrums, calling yourself my victim, accusing him. He knows you tried to kill me.

—Lying. More lying. It's all you know, Dim. If I

wasn't so fucking angry I'd feel sorry for you. Suicide's an easy way out. You must be as sorry as I am that it didn't work.

—No need for pity. I'm the winner, you'll see.

She'd hung up. I *am* the winner. Even though I spoke too soon. I didn't think that it was possible to lose Sly in one of the endings. But surely my own survival is worth something? At the very least, I lived to tell the tale.

Was that end sequence the most luridly lit sequence of events in my life? Was it the end sequence to end all end sequences? If the cat has nine lives then you know the answer.

Quiet now, I'm still telling it. No whispering, no quibbling over detail. Listen. There in the heart of the pyramid, Sly's talking.

—Dim. So aptly named. Not that you're slow in any way. It's just where you live. A half-light hangs over you. I never loved anyone the way I love you.

Side by side we lie on the bed, poised just above the piles of sand drifted at the heart of the pyramid, still not cleared after the terrors of Lock's dust storm. Parts of the sand have solidified into a kind of concrete where they were doused in Cell's tsunami.

I knew Sly was worrying about the madness that had subsumed me and Cell. He could see that all this opposition was concentrating towards evil. We were pushed there, all three of us. He couldn't help tracing it back to me. It was like I brought it with me, this Pandora's box saved from some wreckage, grappled to the childlike frame of my shipwrecked soul as I clutched at

Cell's tidal passage with a near annihilated determination. She brought me in, brought me back to life, chafed my iciness into presence. And before we knew it, something was telling me to open up my little box and its frightening histories in a perverse game of show and tell. He couldn't believe that my seeming innocence had unleashed such darkness. He didn't want to think about it, so he changed the topic.

—Sometimes I think that I've never heard you, Dim. As if you've never consciously told me anything. But in the subtlest reaches of my thinking are the trails of you, like tracings on a scribbly bark tree.

Sly is talking for the sake of it. I can tell it comforts him, as it does me, to hear the melodious furnishing of space which his voice can effect. Underneath, he doesn't know what to do or what to say or where to start with any of it. There's so much anger and debris that he feels caught in chaos. He is at a loss to know what to do about Cell. He won't let go of me because he can't let go of his cherished idea of a child. He's made up his mind to hang on for the next four months, when the deadlock will break and he can sort the whole mess out. He's confident about this. But meanwhile there is the pressure of Cell's dissolution.

—I really do think she's gone mad. And don't get me wrong. I don't mean that it's your fault.

I surprise him by answering him.

—There's only the huge hiatus that is created when yin and yang fly apart and a huge swallow of void takes over.

It must be in response to this image of severance and apocalypse that he wants to come inside me. An instinctive reaction.

Usually when I lay under Sly I was a spectator. I would watch him make love to me as if I was at the drive-in. He was technicoloured and larger than life, and his voice crowded my ears. I prostrated myself to him as to a deity.

But this night is different. Perhaps for the first time I stop dancing around the screen, playing games with the image of desire as it looms so large before me, blurring on the edge of focus as the frames unfold concertina-like and we wait for the huge grainy resolution and the lights coming on to signal the end. Something arrests me, makes me stop my elusive nonsense. This time I creep near to the place where he has intense expression, and suddenly I am drawn up to the surface of the screen. I make contact—there is light and mottled colour on my hands where they have touched his enormous melting face. Do I cry out? Perhaps that's why his mouth descends like a hot-air balloon and bears me up into the skies on the other side of the surface. It is an annunciation, but once there with him I find his voice is only a beautiful illusion, a trick of soundwaves pulsating on air, no power except the power of beauty and even though my idol is cast down I am not because I am superseding, speeding to another place where *I* am the voice that makes it all mean something. Astonished tiny me, clutching for safety up there where the clouds shine out ecstasy and the world cries out take me and the light is pulsing white to yellow to orange.

And suddenly everything is on fire. Literally everything is on fire. That Cell, torching my destiny. Cell? Is she there, you ask? You want refinement, facts, detail. You want to know who is there. O but it is a valid question! The answer though, is not predictable. The answer is perhaps someone completely unanticipated.

Is it Cell, the madwoman burning the house down? Or is it the Warlock, the spurned lover and wicked wolf, scourging his faithless and sullied monster-bride, huffing and puffing and blowing her pyramid down? Or is it just me, self-immolating, bringing myself to term? It is true that all of us, Morgan's players, are there, Cell and Lock and Sly and Dim, in the crucible together. But who can say which of us is precipitating this end sequence, the penultimate death that gives me to you? If anything, we are all responsible. Truly, my only chance here is to lose everything, in the hope that I just might lose Morgan in the process, evaporated away forever in a belch of hideous sulphuric fumes.

Now I can unstitch you. I am no longer scared of the competing voices because it is far too late for any of that now. Benign, I stretch out my needle and pick each thread loose, careful not to jab or wound your punished face, working fast because I don't want you to miss anything. Your eyes pop open, your lips though chapped gape and flex. You burst your bonds and you are as alive and as free as Cell and you can judge me. But there is only so much of that me left for you to pronounce on, and just as you seek and find me I will have renounced my name and clutched for redemption, and you will be left, always in the weaker position, asking yourself if the person Dimity had it in her to live a winning last life, successfully foiling a curse? Use your eyes, now you've got them back. Watch.

The flames are coming from over Sly's shoulder. I can see my left foot at the end of the bed, my heel up over Sly's calf. The spiral serpent is so black there it is as if it has been burned into the skin. Smoke wreathes it. The spiral serpent curls all its power tight and wards off silence. Can this possibly work? It works enough for me to open my mouth and scream one long slow raking scream to warn Sly that the fire is coming for him.

I remember this. I remember the scorching smells of synthetics burning. I remember the smoke, veining lungs in torture. I remember the bodies writhing in the red flower, howling with pain. I have been in this volcano before, more than once.

Sly is trying to escape. Is there escape?

—Come on, Dim, he was saying. Come on Dim come on

And the crude pressure, the dark confinement of being near Christ but sweet Jesus don't swear Morgan would have a fit don't swear don't take it in vain no never anything in vain waiting in vain for your love I don't want to but that's where it always ends up.

And she was. Dim, I mean. A mind battened in by black terrors never get the flare up never shine so bright and she didn't. She died deep in there just ashes now with the faintest breath of heat and light do you think she's dead?

But it's a cave she comes out of. Other names, other Dimitys and she's Mimi some days, with long brown arms like storm-stripped tree branches, naked and beautiful. Survivors. Muscles knotted up in them, growth corded along her. She comes sliding out of penultimate crannies fresh from the slit of earth she's got blood on her hands. And slim as stringy bark reefing off a tall trunk she's dangerous. She's wily and her scared eyes twinkle now with mischief. Can you see her now, waiting at the door of delicious misdemeanour, some long awaited legendary crime with the spirit coming upon her until she's it? The spirit, I mean . . . Standing there like that, she wavers in your gaze.

If she's not real, if she's ephemeral, then that's your funeral. Because even as metaphor she's got the skull and crossbones stamped on her brow. She's secure in that even as she dissolves in air. Evanescent death, her art form.